REBECCA'S STORY

Menopause and Me

Authored by Y L Phillip
©Copyright Y L Phillip 2023

Cover Design: Spiffing Publishing
Edited: Kristine Simelda
Copy Edit: Abbie Starling

Published by Hibiscus-Rose Books
Paperback ISBN: 9781739576608

All rights reserved 2023.

The author asserts the moral right to be identified as the author of this work of fiction. The author created the names and characters in this book; any similarity to real-life events is coincidental.

This book is sold subject to the conditions that it is not, by trade or otherwise, lent, hired out or otherwise circulated in any form of binding or cover other than that in which it is published. No part of this publication may be reproduced, stored in a retrieval system or transmitted in any form or by any means (electronic, mechanical, photocopying, recording or otherwise) without prior written permission from the Author or Publisher.

REBECCA'S STORY

Menopause and Me

Y L PHILLIP

To my dearest husband, daughters, and grandchildren—love, live, laugh, skip, hop, jump, sing and dance.

"Love is patient, love is kind. It does not envy, it does not boast, it is not proud. It is not rude, it is not self-seeking, it is not easily angered, it keeps no record of wrongs. Love does not delight in evil but rejoices with the truth. It always protects, always trusts, always hopes, always perseveres. Love never fails."
1 Corinthians 13: 4-8 New Testament

Acknowledgements:

Thank you to everyone who has made this book come to fruition:

My family—descendants of Ama Rose Commodore, love you to the max. Forward We Go.

Kristine Simelda, my editor, for your commitment, truthfulness, patience, and humour.

Abbie Starling for copy editing and proofreading.

Spiffing Covers for copy editing, proofreading and book cover design.

My friends whose names are too numerous to mention.

Our Newham NHS Reunion group, thank you for your support and sharing your stories. Take each day at a time.

Y L Phillip

Chapter 1
Godiva Veiled in Black

Rebecca places her foot in the stirrup and confidently hoists herself on the back of a temperamental chestnut stallion. In her dream, they gallop through the village like she is Lady Godiva, covered by a black veil. Rebecca holds her head high as bystanders dive out of the way. With the reins in one hand, she raises the other fist in defiance as the horse pounds down the dusty road.

"I'm not afraid of you, Hot Flushes!" she shouts, pointing at the onlookers. "Back off, you cowards: Frustration, Anxiety, Perspiration, Sleeplessness, Depression, Mood Swings, Fatigue and Memory Loss! So what if I've temporarily lost my Libido?"

The horse picks up his pace and then suddenly veers off course. When the sweat-soaked stallion stops abruptly and rears on its hind legs, Rebecca loses her balance and slides from the saddle. To her horror, her foot gets caught in a stirrup. She is dragged through the village while the spectators jeer at her predicament.

Defiant, Rebecca untangles the stirrup, gets a running start and vaults onto the back of the ruthless horse.

Screaming whilst kneeling on her bed, with arms extended, Rebecca emulates an amateur horse rider holding the reins tightly, trying to tame a wild horse. With teeth protruding, nose flaring and eyes bulging, Rebecca confidently wraps the reins around four fingers.

"I am not afraid of you!" she shouts at the stallion. Tossing and turning in her sleep, she wakes up, and frantically kicks her feet as if to free them. Punching the air, she liberates herself from the sheets, stumbles out of bed, and opens the bedroom windows wide.

Panting, Rebecca regards the dreary London skies and contemplates the meaning of her dream. She's never been on a horse and isn't interested in showing strangers her ageing body. Drawing in a breath, Rebecca considers the nature of the trauma she is going through. She remembers her grandmother and her friends holding the hems of their dresses and fanning themselves whilst chatting nonchalantly about the heat of older women. Rebecca did not take notice at that time, nor when her mother complained about the "blasted heat". She did not realise that she, Rebecca, would feel its force.

"OW!" Rebecca groans, exhaling. "When will it end?" Unbearably hot, sweaty, and agitated, she angrily removes her soaked nightdress, throws it in the linen basket, showers, and changes into fresh clothes.

Cross with herself that she's sweating again, she returns to the window for fresh air. Rebecca believes a dream reveals something significant about the future and wonders what this one could mean. Fretfully, she considers how she might duck the impending disaster.

When Rebecca fails to reach a reasonable conclusion, she decides to have a cup of tea. She worries while the kettle boils and then walks back to her bedroom with a steaming mug in hand. In an attempt at distraction, Rebecca focuses on the cooking she plans to do later. She has already seasoned her meats and left them to marinate in the fridge overnight. Her kidney beans are soaking, so what could possibly go wrong? *Positivity all the way!* So says one of the affirmations hanging on the green wall in the kitchen.

It's Sunday morning, so Rebecca doesn't have to go to work at school. She lingers in her favourite armchair and recalls painful events in the past. Shutting her eyes, Rebecca reflects on her life with her children. She wishes she had done more for them when they were young. Tears run down her cheeks as she thinks about the plight of her son, RD, who was sentenced to prison for attempted murder because of mistaken identity. Of course, he wasn't guilty, but she's angry because years passed while no one did anything to try to get him out. But when she thinks of how RD is now—a valued member of the community whose life positively impacts young peoples' future—Rebecca smiles.

Her daughter, Shantel, is another story. The muscles in her face tighten as she thinks about how sharp tongues condemned both her and her daughter when times were tough. Shantel was a teenage mother who was so embarrassed by her condition that she concealed her pregnancy until the last moment. But certain people felt that as a mother and a teacher, "That clever Rebecca should have known better."

"If only," she sighs. That was ten years ago, and Rebecca nods as she thinks about how Shantel has matured. She's a teacher like her, and her son Phoenix is a delight. They have such a good grandmother-to-grandson relationship. Rebecca enjoys spending time with Phoenix, talking and playing Maths games with him. (He says he wants to be the Chancellor of the Exchequer when he grows up.) She also loves listening to him read his poems and stories and encourages him to write more. Looking up to heaven, she thanks God for her exceptional grandson.

Slowly, Rebecca's eyelids meet. Her chin drops to her chest as she fights off sleep. Her head bounces up and down, but eventually, exhaustion wins due to such a restless night. A few hours later, she is startled as the cup smashes on the floor and the cold tea splashes on her feet. She jumps up from the chair and stares at the clock. Her deep sighs and glance at her face in the mirror even startles her. "My goodness. Look at the time. I'd better start cooking before my son rings the doorbell and no food is ready. Yes, my dear. RD loves his mama's Creole cooking, and I don't want to disappoint him."

Chapter 2

Feeling Hot, Hot, Hot

Rebecca stares at the green wall behind the table when she enters the kitchen. One of the many framed affirmations hanging on it reads: *When life gives you lemons, make lemonade.* She smiles at the huge bowl of lemons, oranges, bananas and mangoes in the middle of her drop-leaf table. Feeling flushed, she cracks the windows to let in some cool air.

After taking the Tupperware containers out of the fridge, she places two spotlessly scrubbed Dutch pots on the hobs protruding through the piece of foil on her cooker. Rebecca doesn't want any spillage—she's not in the mood to spend ages cleaning up a mess. Separating the meat from the onion and garlic marinade, she browns it. She adds water to the marinade in another pot and allows it to boil. Whistling gleefully, she pours the contents of both vessels into another Dutch pot. Rebecca adds copious amounts of curry powder, paprika, turmeric, sprigs of thyme, some cloves, four cloves of garlic, onions and her own special seasoning. She samples the content, and satisfied, she leaves the meat to stew.

Rebecca drains the water from the kidney beans and refreshes them with cold water and salt. Then she turns on the cooker full blast. She plans to turn down the fire when it starts to boil but gets distracted by the troublesome dream about the chestnut stallion she had last night. Lost in space, she is unaware that the pot's water is boiling over. Rushing towards the cooker, Rebecca's eyes widen as the brownish, red liquid bubbles and spills over the side of the pot onto the foil. Turning the fire down, Rebecca chews on her bottom lip in concentration. She then crushes more cloves of garlic and tosses them, along with an intact scotch bonnet pepper, into the beans. She is impressed with her foil's protection and wipes the cooker clean with a damp cloth.

Smiling, she looks at her face in the shiny splash back. With puckered lips, Rebecca sings, "Ole Ole Ole Ole …" Rebecca dances with the wooden spoon in the air. "RD and Phoenix are bound to love my Caribbean recipe for rice and peas," she declares. "I may be a basket case, but I can still cook."

Humming with happiness, she puts the washed rice into the pot of kidney beans and sets it to boil. "Feelin' hot, hot, hot," she sings, tapping the wooden spoon on the granite worktop and then the salad bowl. As Rebecca prepares the salad, her nostrils register a melee of scents—spring onion, sweet peppers, and garlic dressing. Now that everything is in order, she returns to her room to resume reading her book, *The Alchemist*. "Like me, Santiago is on a journey," she says out loud. "I wonder what he will go through as he embarks on his journey."

The aroma of the food wafts through the kitchen window whilst her son RD stands at the back door. His mouth waters as he inhales the smells. He has his keys in hand, but as usual, he insists on ringing the doorbell. Rebecca has warned him before to use his key; right now, she cannot be bothered to open the door for him again. Preoccupied with her thoughts, Rebecca ignores the bell.

RD eventually gives up and inserts his key. As her son enters the kitchen, he screws up his face and rubs his nose with disappointment. The pleasant aroma of food infused with aromatic Caribbean herbs and spices has changed to the unpleasant smell of burning rice. His lower lip drops. He was looking forward to his mother's home-cooked meal, but she seems to have forgotten to lower the fire. RD moves out of the way as his mother pounds down the stairs and rushes into the kitchen. Grimacing, she pulls the scalding pot barehanded from the hob and flings it onto a metal table outside. RD covers his ears at the deafening sound it makes when it connects. He feels sorry for the revered flowerpot his mother has had since time immemorial as the uncaring Dutch pot smashes it to smithereens.

Pinching his nose to prevent inhaling the smoke, he puts on the fan above the cooker. As his hand touches the pots and hanging utensils, they bash into each other, causing even more ruckus. Meanwhile, Rebecca runs. She stops. Her eyes dart back and forth. She grabs a placement mat and frantically runs around the house, fanning her nose. Mumbling under her breath, she pushes the rest of the windows open wide. RD's mum, who is usually focused and proud to be following "the family recipes passed down to her by her mother, whose mother passed them down to her," is irritable and cursing under her breath.

"Mum, what's going on with you today? Why did you forget what you were doing and burn the rice and peas? That's not like you."

RD's mother doesn't respond. She seems miles away, her face tense, her nostrils flickering, and her lips pressed together. She shuts one eye and stands in front of the cooker. "That's not a very good commendation for your dear old mum, is it, RD?" she says.

He studies Rebecca as she rubs her curled finger back and forth over her upper lip. "Are you okay, Mum?" he asks her.

"Questions, questions, and more questions," she grumbles. "I'm trying to figure out where I put the cheese to make the macaroni, and you …"

"You've not made the macaroni cheese yet?" RD

asks in desperation. His belly rumbles loudly.

Defiantly, Rebecca's brow creases. "No. You bombard me with questions which confuse and distract me." Rebecca gives him her back and turns on one of the many fans in the house. She stands in front of it and leans forward to clear her head.

When she reaches into the food cupboard, RD questions her yet again. "If you're looking for the cheese, Mum, shouldn't it be in the fridge?"

Scratching her head, Rebecca stands perplexed and in despair, but she says nothing. Trying not to show embarrassment, she hides the cheese in a tea towel, transferring it from the cupboard into the fridge like it was always there. Secretly, she wonders why she put it in the cupboard, but then she decides that someone else must have done it.

RD stares at his mother. She is pulling her top off her shoulders and fanning it up and down. "Puff! Puff!" she blows to diffuse the unwarranted attention. Rebecca stands in front of the fan with her head almost touching it as the extreme heat spreads up her neck to her face and head. Perspiration drips off the tip of her nose while RD offers his hankie in empathy. As she silently curses, the tyrant backs off, and the sweat shower dries up without apologising. She puts on a cardigan and stands in front of the fridge, shivering.

"Are you okay, Mum?" RD asks again. He stares at his mother in confusion as she takes the cardigan off and puts it back on. "Where else could you have put the cheese?" he says, searching the fridge. "Mum, it's right here!" RD picks it up and shows it to his mother.

Her look says it all. "I could have sworn I checked in the fridge, but the cheese wasn't there," she says guiltily.

RD follows her exaggerated movements as she opens the cupboard door. CRASH! The pots and pans bellow in pain as they scatter onto the floor.

RD covers his ears again while Rebecca retrieves yet another Dutch pot. "How many of these do you have, Mum?" he asks. He tries to make a joke. "It seems like you should open a business and call it 'Rebecca's Dutch Pots.' Don't you think?" He laughs, but she doesn't join in.

Mumbling under her breath, Rebecca noisily washes the pots and pans and replaces them in the cupboard. RD leaves the kitchen due to the chaos, but he returns moments later to offer her his help. She looks at her son with such irritation that RD steps back. He watches as his mother pours lentils into the latest pot, and his sensitive ears tingle as they drop into the pan.

Hastily, Rebecca fills the pot with water, and it splashes as she vigorously rinses the lentils. She pours the water, and it washes away some lentils scattered in the sink. The other pots bang together in disharmony as Rebecca reaches for the next pan hanging above her head. She fills it with cold water and puts it on the hob.

With matches in hand, she turns the knob but does not light the cooker. RD stares at her while the hissing gas escapes. He is about to turn off the knob but quickly retracts his hands because of the intimidating grimaces on his mother's face as she intervenes. Coming back to earth, she kisses her teeth and finally cracks a match. WHOOSH!

Forcefully, Rebecca cuts her eyes at RD and clips back her curly weave to avoid an accidental singeing. She washes her hands and adds some lemon slices to another pot of boiling water.

RD smiles as he reads the same affirmation about lemonade on the green wall. Assuming his mum is making a pot of lemon tea, RD cuts a piece of her famous carrot, lemon, and ginger cake and puts it on a plate in anticipation. Rubbing his neck, he's surprised when she puts the pot and its lemon contents in the corner of the kitchen.

"What are you doing, Mum? Aren't you making lemon tea?" he asks.

Rebecca's face is tense. "Questions, questions, Rowan." RD knows his mum is upset once she calls him by that name. "Why don't you stop asking so many questions? Burnt, innit!" Rebecca shouts. His mother's violent reaction startles him. RD follows her into another room, where she stands in front of yet another fan.

"I did that with the lemons to eliminate the burnt smell," she says indignantly.

"Okay," he tells her. "Today, I've learnt something new."

She smiles for the first time since he's entered the house. "It's never too late, RD."

"What's never too late?" Shantel asks as she opens the back door wider. In normal circumstances, she would have alerted the firefighters immediately by dialling 999.

Still, she knows that her mum "has done it again," so she isn't in a hurry to do anything so drastic.

Shantel eyes her mother with concern. Shaking her scarf up and down repeatedly, she says, "Not again, Mum." Rebecca's daughter, who lives at home, is becoming increasingly concerned about her mum's recurrent burning of food and her impatience, bad mood and intolerance when questioned about it.

Shantel's son Phoenix fans his face with his cap and hugs Rebecca reassuringly. "It's okay, Grandma," he says as she storms out of the kitchen.

Shantel shakes her head. "What happened, RD? You're helping Mum to burn the food, or what?"

"If I burned the food, that would be reasonable, but Mum is usually so proud of her cooking."

"I know."

"So, what's going on, Shantel? Why does she keep burning the food?"

Rebecca walks back into the kitchen and scowls at her adult children. Having overheard what she takes as criticism, she folds her arms, tightens her lips, and retreats to her bedroom. Taking her meal with her, she leaves her children and grandson to eat without her.

Deep in conversation, RD and Shantel reflect on their mum's love, compassion, and concern for them. They are grateful. They love her dearly and want the best for her. They appreciate every meal she cooked "with her own hands" for them. RD drools as he remembers the tantalising taste of his mother's cooked saltfish and fried plantain with hard dough bread, but today, they wonder what happened.

"My grandma is awesome. Grandma is the best cook in the world," Phoenix says as he finishes his food. He takes a piece of hard dough bread and wipes his plate clean. He eats the bread, rubs his belly, burps and says, "Mmm! I love Grandma and her cooking. She's the best." He gulps down a glass of his grandmother's homemade ginger beer. As he leaves the table to play his Maths game, the radio plays "Simply The Best" by Tina Turner.

As Shantel listens to the song, she slowly removes her hands from her guilt-ridden face. But she doesn't feel as bad when she looks at her brother as he adds copious amounts of hot pepper sauce to his food and chews it with distaste. "Should I? Shall I? Well, I'm going to say it anyway. I'm not enjoying Mum's meal today, RD. I usually eat the chicken thighs down to the bones and even suck the marrow out of them," she puckers her lips and pulls the air through her mouth without using her teeth. "But Bro, today, it's a challenge," Shantel says.

"Sis, I feel bad, but what you say is true. My taste buds normally dance with enjoyment when eating Mum's food, but today, they're disappointed. My mouth was about to shout, "Rebecca! What the hell happened?" but my teeth held my tongue captive, and because of my love for my mum, Sis, I didn't disrespect her. I'm not enjoying the food either, but I know Mum tries so hard to make sure what she cooks pleases us, so I'm trying to eat some." RD adds more pepper sauce and some Levi Roots Reggae Reggae Jerk BBQ Sauce.

"Let the truth be told, RD, but don't let our mother hear you. Don't let her see you, either."

Shantel and RD struggle to eat the remainder of their meals. RD, who normally takes some food home in a Tupperware container, declines. "Not today, Tups," he tells the container. "I'll be leaving without you, sorry." Shantel laughs. RD surveys the doorway to ensure his mother is not standing there, stops eating, and consequently scrapes the food onto a newspaper and places it in the bin. "Au revoir," he waves.

"Saying goodbye to the scraps in French, Bro? You cannot be serious."

RD laughs out loud as he looks at an old photo of his mum and thinks of the woman who stood at his bedroom door when he was a kid. She had a hood pulled on her head and bobbed up and down like one of the teenagers at the community centre, rapping to her heart's content.

"What is so funny?" Shantel asks. "Is it Mum's disastrous cooking?"

"Not that, Shantel! I did not enjoy it, but I wouldn't disrespect Mum like that. Just remembering how our mum was before and the antics she got up to. She made us laugh most of the time despite the troubles she was going through with Dad. Do you remember when she used to dress up and rap like a teenager and ask us if we liked her swagger?"

Shantel laughs, "Yeah, Bro. She was hilarious. She used to make me crease up with laughter." Shantel looks at Rebecca's photo. "I can see her dancing to the Soca music, lifting her leg up, whining her waist and giggling, and singing at the top of her voice. "Who let the dogs out? Who, who, who, who …" She demonstrates, and RD laughs and barks. "Bro, where has all the vivaciousness gone? Where has Rebecca gone? I feel so sorry for her now. I love our Angel."

"I love her too, Sis. I know better days will come, and Mum will be herself again," RD says, clasping his hands in prayer. He raps "Better Days Will Come" to Le'Andria Johnson's song lyrics, and Shantel joins him, tapping her fork on the side of her nearly full plate.

Phoenix hears the music playing, and he returns to the dining room. He does not like rapping, but he nods his head to each bar. There is no sign of Rebecca.

RD goes to his mother's bedroom to say goodbye. Then, RD retracts his lip when he hears her praying, asking God to encourage her children to be more mindful of her predicament. Mindfully, he does not disturb her.

Chapter 3

Dungeons of the Past

After a disappointing dinner, Rebecca sits pensively in the corner of her dark room. Her lips are tight, and her cheeks are inflated. She crosses her arm across her chest tightly. She's displeased by her children's conversation behind her back and their "ungratefulness" for what she has done for them "all by herself." She attempts to iron out the creases in her forehead with her hands as she reflects on her life as a single parent. Imprisoned in the dungeon of her past life—her emotional abuse by her husband, his physical abuse of RD, and her initial disappointment in Shantel—she must dig deep down to find comfort.

The poorly cooked lentils have given her gas, and Rebecca has trouble sleeping again. This time, she has a different dream. She wakes up startled and shouts, "Rowan! Where are you?" Jumping up from the bed, she searches the corners and crevices of the room as if she's looking for her son. "What has he done to you?" she wails desperately. "Put him down! He's just a boy!"

Sweat drips down her back as she raises her arms and repeatedly punches the air like she's confronting a ghost.

She is irritable, hot, and soaked in sweat. She wakes up several times to change her clothing and bed linen. Eventually exhausted, Rebecca manages to resume much-needed sleep, but after a short while, her phone alarm rings. It's midnight, so she must have set it to the wrong time. Confused and disorientated, Rebecca pushes the snooze button instead of turning it off. When the alarm goes off again, she is dreaming. The chestnut horse stands over her, blowing hot air into her face. "Argh," Rebecca moans, wiping sweat from her forehead. Rebecca kicks the covers off, takes off her night dress, and pushes the window above the bed out in frustration. "That blasted heat! What's the point of wearing Victoria's Secret when you sweat right through the lace?"

She tries to go back to sleep, but there is too much confusion in her head.

Like a time bomb, Rebecca's mind goes a mile a minute while her thoughts race from one subject to another. She can feel the heat rising from her neck to her head. Her throat feels tight, so she sits up, takes controlled breaths, and puts the fan and the bedside light on. Unable to sleep, Rebecca goes into her kitchen and puts some water to boil. In it, she adds grated cocoa, a bay leaf, a cinnamon stick, grated nutmeg and leaves to boil. Her eyes are focused on the hob, and she is mindful that it does not boil over. She does not want another disaster. Satisfied, she adds Carnation milk and some sugar to the pot. Rebecca prays for a good night's sleep while drinking her warm cup of cocoa, but that doesn't help. She attempts to read a book, but she can't concentrate. She tries counting sheep instead, but that's no good.

With the white of her eyes conspicuous, Rebecca stares at the clock on the wall, monitoring every second that ticks by. She points at it and rotates her finger anti-clockwise, wishing she could turn back time. Rebecca has no regrets about having her children but wishes the circumstances had changed. If she had married another man—one who was caring, compassionate, and respectful—life would have been better. "If only I'd had a supportive husband, a man who loved his whole family and not just his daughter. But life is what it is." Pensive, Rebecca closes her eyes and imagines Doris Day singing "Whatever Will Be, Will Be" and joins in.

"Que sera sera

Whatever will be, will be

The future's not ours to see.

Que sera sera

Whatever will be will be …"

Tucking the sheet around her like a baby swaddled, Rebecca drifts to sleep, but as soon as she's settled, her nemesis gallops into the room with his teeth exposed. Rebecca's heart rate increases as her arms are in all directions to protect her. She moves out of the way, but the horse charges at her and paws at Rebecca with hooves that are burning hot. Rebecca prays for the horse in her dreams to leave her alone, but the heat is unbearable.

That blasted horse is getting on my nerves. This constant sweating is tiresome and disturbs my sleep. Dear Lord, when will this stop? When will I get peace?

She flings the cover off her. "This is relentless!" she groans.

Rebecca wakes up to the ringing of the clock alarm for the second time.

"Already? It's Monday morning. Don't tell me I have to get up so early." Though she's naked, she's drenched in sweat. Her heart is galloping. "When am I going to get a good night's sleep?"

She kicks off the covers, breathes in and out slowly and lays there for a while. Before she picks her discarded night dress up from the floor beside the bed, Rebecca clenches her teeth in anger. "This constant putting on and taking off is bloody annoying. I'm under the covers one minute and on top the next. And that dream—where did that chestnut horse come from?" she asks in exasperation.

Yawning, Rebecca gradually rolls onto her side. Pressing her hand on the bed, she pushes herself up. Sitting on the edge of the mattress, her mind is bombarded with disturbing questions and unlikely solutions. Her knees creak like a rickety old chair when she stands, but she commands them to behave because she will need them to support her for the rest of the day. She takes a tube of Voltarol from the bedside table, rubs her knees vigorously, and then drops a pillow on the floor. "Ooh," she groans as she kneels and clasps her hands in prayer.

Rebecca prays for world peace and harmony. Then she asks the Almighty for the good health of all her family and friends, also for RD, hoping he will find a wife soon. She prays for Shantel and hopes that she and Silk will reconcile and that Phoenix will do well in all aspects of his life. Rebecca prays for the strength of the community—that the young people will love and respect each other and that they will converse with the older generation in meaningful dialogue. "With respect comes love, and with love comes respect," Rebecca says.

Lastly, she prays that she will find herself soon and those hot flushes disappear. "Please, God, heal my aching knees and free me from these annoying hot flushes and this blasted stallion."

Angered, the horse responds by snorting a blast of heat inside her body. "Take that!" he says. But God must have heard her prayer because, to Rebecca's relief, the beast calms down after a few moments.

"Ouch!" Rebecca groans in pain as she stands. She rubs her knees with more Voltarol, preparing them for their task. "Ahhh," she says, "that feels good." She goes to the kitchen, makes herself a cup of green tea, and returns to her room to get ready for work. But as she sits in the chair beside the bed, Rebecca is once more consumed by disturbing thoughts. Lost in her own story, she contemplates the reasons and consequences of her divorce. Her eyes fill with tears thinking about young RD and the physical abuse he suffered at his father's angry hands. Covering her eyes, she cannot get the vision of what happened out of her head. Digging her fingers into her scalp, Rebecca attempts to pick out answers to her questions.

What else should I have done to protect my son? Why did it take me so long to find out my husband had been beating him in private? Why didn't Rowan tell me sooner? What kind of mother was I? The abuse would have continued if I hadn't gotten Blake out of my life.

Thinking about Shantel, she wonders how she missed the fact that her daughter was concealing her pregnancy.

How could I have overlooked that, too? Was I so consumed by my own problems that I didn't realise things had got to the point of no return? Could I not see the woods for the trees?

When Rebecca thinks about her experience of being emotionally abused by her husband, shame overwhelms her. Her body tightens, her breathing increases, and she crosses her arms to protect herself from her husband's ghost.

Why did I stay in that relationship for so long? I should

have acted sooner.

Feeling stressed, Rebecca squeezes her eyes tightly shut. She leans back in the chair, remembering what her counsellor, Mr Xavier, told her when RD was in prison: *Don't beat yourself up, Rebecca. You did all you could with the tools you had at the time.* Rebecca sighs and sits up because her body suddenly feels on fire, and her nightdress is again soaked with sweat. She takes it off and avoids looking in the mirror. The reflection of her naked body would do nothing to lift her spirits.

Chapter 4
Asking for Help

While recovering from the latest hot flush, Rebecca reflects on her conversations with Shantel about the possibility of going through menopause (aka the "change" and "that thing") and how she denied the possible need to contact a doctor for help. "It is just a phase in my life that I must go through. It will pass soon," she told her daughter. "I think I'm going through the change. Don't worry." Rebecca feels that she can manage its brutal attack by herself. She has numerous leaflets about "that thing" and how to deal with it. *I'll wait a while longer and contact my doctor when I can no longer cope.* But now that "that thing" has repeatedly attacked her in private and also embarrassed her in public, she has had enough. "We are locked in battle, and I cannot let the brute win," she professes. "The brute must go."

Rebecca is so distressed that she calls in sick to work. She hates doing this but will be useless at school unless she gets some relief, so she calls her doctor for advice. Someone else has cancelled; fortunately, she gets an appointment during lunchtime.

Huffing and puffing, Rebecca grabs her bag, flask and flannel and slams the front door behind her. Opening the car window wide, she talks incessantly to herself until she arrives at her destination. She pleads to "that thing" to give her a break. She hopes her doctor will offer the proper treatment to relieve her from "that thing".

Rebecca slams the car door shut and advances up the stairs with vigour. She is hot and flustered as she charges to the reception desk at her GP practice. The other people waiting patiently to see the doctor are alerted to the tapping sound from her shoes. Glaring at the receptionist, Rebecca wipes the sweat dripping from her chin and the tip of her nose several times with an already-soaked flannel. "I'm here to see Dr um, um, Lily," Rebecca says. She is asked to wait, and she is not impressed.

"But I'm here on time for my appointment," she says, looking at the clock behind the desk and gulping cold water from her flask. She is hot, bothered and overwhelmed by her symptoms. So, she wants to see her doctor. In desperation, she asks, "Why can't she see me now?"

"I'm sorry, Mrs Dawson, but Dr Lily is running late. She will see you as soon as she can," says the receptionist, looking at Rebecca's drenched face and top.

Impatient, Rebecca paces in the waiting room as she awaits her turn. She returns a few times to the desk and enquires how long she has to wait. She rolls her eyes in annoyance. *Tell her what you're thinking about the long wait. Tell her it is unacceptable. Give her a piece of your mind for not being seen sooner,* her head tells her, but her mouth refuses to speak. Rebecca is grateful that Dr Lily will see her at short notice, so she holds her tongue.

It is Rebecca's turn. *About time!* She thinks as she enters Dr Lily's office.

"Good afternoon, Mrs Dawson. Sorry about the wait. Please sit."

"Thank you," she says, fanning the flannel back and forth to cool her down.

"What can I do for you?" Dr Lily asks.

Rebecca wipes her forehead, neck, and chest and puffs out like she is blowing a huge candle. Silently, Dr Lily observes Rebecca and gives her time to speak. She has noticed this behaviour in many women of Rebecca's age, but she wants to hear Rebecca's story.

"Are you okay, Mrs Dawson? Can you tell me how you're feeling?"

"I've had enough. I cannot take this anymore. This thing is so damn annoying. Sorry, Dr Lily. Excuse my bad manners. Good afternoon. One minute, I'm hot; the next, I'm cold. I'm hot, frustrated, anxious and irritable. I sweat all night, and I cannot sleep." Rebecca yawns. "My heart beats fast, and my breathing is erratic. I cannot understand what is happening to my body. This bothers me. I need something to help me. I need to sleep. I don't know what to do. I cannot take this anymore."

"Okay, I hear you. Tell me more about what is bothering you," Dr Lily says.

"The hot flushes are miserable. The sweating does not stop. I constantly have to put the fan on and then off, and then on again. This is really frustrating. I have to change my clothes often. The washing is unrelenting."

"I understand," the doctor says sympathetically, nodding for Rebecca to continue.

Frustrated, Rebecca scratches her head. "And I have ..." Rebecca closes her eyes momentarily, rubs her forehead and opens them again. "What's it called again? Um, um, brain fog."

"Brain fog? Can you tell me more about this?"

"Yeah. My brain feels like cotton wool. I find it difficult to take in and remember information. I sometimes struggle to find the word I need to complete a sentence when I speak. Am I going out of my mind Dr Lily?"

Dr Lily is attentive. She wants to hear more to help her with her diagnosis. So, she lets Rebecca continue.

"I sometimes struggle to remember what I want to say and do; even if I make a list, I forget the list. I forget people's names, even my neighbours. I burn the food. Can you imagine that?" Rebecca says, her eyes are welling up in tears. Dr Lily hands her a tissue. "I am listening," she reassures Rebecca.

Rebecca nods, but her face is tense. "I cannot retain information. I am a teacher, after all. What good am I if I cannot impart …" Scrunching her lips and squinting, she prays to God to find the word … "Knowledge? That isn't good, is it? Dr Lily, I forgot to spell the name of the road where I live. I felt like a fool." Rebecca is silent momentarily as she remembers how embarrassed she was when she had to return to the florist to give her the correct spelling of her address.

"I'm listening," Dr Lily says.

"It is so frustrating. I constantly apologise for my sweaty hands, arms, face, neck and back. It is really embarrassing. Can you imagine having to say, sorry, I'm sweating. Look at my wet hands, Dr Lily." Rebecca opens the palms of her hands wide and stretches them towards Dr Lily. She retracts them and wipes her hands with her flannel.

"Yes, I can see that, Mrs Dawson."

"Can you imagine how I feel when people reach out to shake my hands? Inside, I'm usually nervous but reluctant, I oblige. I can't refuse, can I? But, Dr Lily, can you imagine how I feel when they retract their hands or surreptitiously wipe them? It is so demoralising. And, um, um … Oh, gosh! It's happening again!" Her breathing is erratic. She cups her head in her hands.

"Brain fog?"

"No. That heat! That intolerable heat! It comes from nowhere, without warning," Rebecca pants and tugs at her top.

"Take a deep breath and breathe out slowly. One, two, three, four, five, and again. One, two, three, four, five. That's it. You're doing well, Mrs Dawson. Stay calm. Can you feel the difference?"

"Yes, I actually can."

"That's a good way to deal with your hot flushes." Dr Lily advises. She then advises Rebecca to wear cotton clothing and dress in layers as she can take some off easily at the start of a hot flush. Also, she must carry a portable fan when the hot flushes attack.

"Do you still have a menstrual period?" Dr Lily asks.

"Do I?" Rebecca says with some sarcasm. "I bleed heavily and even leak through my sanitary towels onto my clothing. It's so embarrassing. I wear black clothing all the time."

"Does the bleeding stop you from doing your normal activities?"

"No, Dr Lily. It is just annoying." Rebecca sighs.

"How long does the bleeding lasts?"

"Four to five days, and that's too long," Rebecca pulls a face.

"It would be a good idea to keep a diary of your periods and how many pads you use. We can look at the diary at your next visit to determine whether you need to be tested for bleeding problems," Dr Lily suggests.

"I'm okay with that, Dr Lily," Rebecca says, fanning herself vigorously and putting her head nearer the fan.

"That's it. You're doing very well." Dr Lily says as Rebecca copes with the hot flush. She then allows Rebecca to speak about her fears, feelings, and anxiety about what she is going through. She listens with empathy and suggests exercises, breathing techniques and coping methods. She ends the discussion by telling Rebecca, "Always make sure you're comfortable before exercising, and breathe in through your mouth and slowly breathe out through your nose. When you breathe in, let your breath flow as deeply into your tummy as is comfortable without forcing it. Like this." She demonstrates, and Rebecca copies. "Mrs Dawson, it is of uttermost importance for you to manage your symptoms of hot flushes. It is good to keep a diary of what triggers your hot flushes, how they affect you, and how you manage them. This will help you decide what treatment you need and how to manage the hot flushes. Management is key," she tells her."

Dr Lily asks Rebecca about her general health and then weighs her, but Rebecca does not look at the scales. She does not want the scales to confirm what she has been thinking. She does not want the scales to compete with her conscience, but the scale asks questions, and her conscience comments.

"Rebecca, what the hell happened?"

"You should have done something earlier to prevent the weight gain."

"Have you not heard about healthy eating and regular exercise?"

"Tut, tut, Rebecca. You should be ashamed of yourself."

"What are you going to do about it?"

"Walk, Rebecca walk. Run Rebecca run. Jump, Rebecca, jump. Jog, Rebecca, jog. Dance, Rebecca, dance."

Rebecca covers her ears to shut the scale and her conscience up.

She focuses on Dr Lily instead as she takes her height, blood pressure and pulse and listens to her chest. They discuss Rebecca's weight and general health, and Dr Lily advises a healthy diet, regular exercise, and a healthy lifestyle. She suggests foods Rebecca should eat to lower her risk of heart disease. "Also, avoiding spicy food, alcohol, and caffeine should help," the doctor advises.

Spicy food, caffeine, and a small amount of Stone's Ginger Wine, now and again? Three of the things I enjoy most. "Okay," Rebecca says, but she knows this is going to be a tough task. "That thing is bothering me, Dr Lily. What is happening to me? Do you think I'm going through the "change"? Or is it something else?" Rebecca asks and is about to jump off her chair when she experiences intense heat across her body and face. She deals with the hot flushes as Dr Lily advised, and she is comfortable again within minutes.

Dr Lily smiles in acknowledgement. "That thing is called hot flushes. You've coped very well with the hot flushes, Mrs Dawson."

"Thank you, Dr Lily," Rebecca smiles.

"You're welcome. You asked about the "change". Many women your age have similar symptoms caused by low hormones in their body when going through menopause, or "change" as it's often called, but there might be other reasons for your symptoms. It's important to find out the exact cause."

"How can we do that?"

"Blood tests can reveal whether or not menopause is the culprit."

"If it's menopause, I've heard that HRT might help with those awful symptoms of menopause," Rebecca says.

Dr Lily nods. "HRT, Hormone Replacement Therapy, is used to treat the symptoms of menopause. It can offer relief for many women from hot flushes, night sweats, and anxiety, Mrs Dawson. Is this something that you would like to consider?"

Jumping up from her seat, Rebecca stands, grabs a magazine on Dr Lily's desk and fans herself. "I feel like I'm inside a furnace," Rebecca says, aiming for the window. She takes some controlled breaths. "I'm not sure about taking HRT. I've heard mixed reviews about it. My friend told me she wouldn't take HRT because of the risk of breast cancer. Is there a risk?"

"Yes, there is a small risk," Dr Lily says, "but the benefits outweigh it. Evidence suggests that HRT can protect you from heart disease and help with bone health."

"That's definitely something to consider."

She hands Rebecca some literature. "You can read more about HRT and menopause, and we can discuss this further at your next appointment if you would like to consider that."

"Thank you. Thank you for listening, Dr Lily."

Dr Lily pats Rebecca on her hand. "You're welcome, Mrs Dawson. I understand what you're going through. Let's take some blood and wait for the blood result, and we can take it from there, but remember what we discussed. Healthy eating, exercising, and maintaining an active lifestyle are very important in helping you cope with the symptoms of menopause, including mood swings. Also, boost your thinking skills by doing activities that enjoyably challenge your brain to help the brain fog. Have you thought about learning to play the piano or playing chess?"

Rebecca scratches her forehead. "I'm too old for that, but I suppose I can give it a go. In the meantime, can you please prescribe me any medication to help relieve my symptoms?" Rebecca tugs at her top and fans herself.

"Yes, I can, but some over-the-counter medications can help. For example, St John's Wort, Evening

Primrose oil and Menopace."

"Menopace? Menopause? I like the sound of that. What does Menopace do?" Rebecca's eyes say it all. *Help me.*

Reading Rebecca's facial gestures, Dr Lily says, "I'm sorry you're going through this." She looks at Rebecca with her eyebrows pulled down flat and forward over the bridge of her nose. Rebecca smiles in acknowledgement and acceptance of Dr Lily's empathy and compassion. "Menopace should help. It is a food supplement you can take during and after menopause. It has vitamin B6, which helps to regulate the activity of the unbalanced hormone in the body. The unbalance of hormones causes those unpleasant symptoms, so Menopace should help." Rebecca smiles. She hopes Menopace will do its magic and soon free her from those dreadful symptoms.

Fanning herself and inhaling and releasing her breath slowly, Rebecca asks. "Does Menopace really work?" She takes a large gulp of ice water from her flask. Then, she pours some water on her flannel and wipes her face.

"Good, Mrs Dawson." Dr Lily says. "It is important to drink water whilst having a hot flush. In fact, it is important to drink about six to eight glasses of fluid every day. Your body needs water to work well."

Rebecca drinks more water while looking for an acknowledgement from her doctor. "I drink about one and a half to two litres daily."

Dr Lily smiles. "That's about right. Answering your question about Menopace, research suggests that Menopace works. It does not contain hormones but has many other vitamins and supplements that provide dietary support during menopause that can help your mental and physical health. Many of my patients swear by it. They say it reduces the incidence of hot flushes and embarrassing sweats."

Hallelujah! Rebecca thinks.

Dr Lily takes some blood from Rebecca. "Here is some information about Menopace. You can try this first and see if it helps. We'll review the results at your next appointment. We should have your blood results by then."

"Okay. Thank you, Dr Lily. I need to feel like myself again. I need to feel comfortable and get on with my life. I need to feel whole again."

"I agree. You deserve to feel your best, Mrs Dawson. So, I'll see you then. In the interim, try and do as I advised, and take care."

Extremely tired, Rebecca tries to sleep, but she dreams of the chestnut stallion again. In her dream, his name is Menopause. Agitated, it sprints towards her with the white of his eyes glaring at her. Frightened, Rebecca dives out of the way, her heart beating quickly. She holds her chest, breathing slowly to calm herself. With composure, she asks the horse to calm down, but it takes no notice. Her heart gallops as the angry horse pins back his ears and swishes his tail. Stomping, squealing and pulling its lip back, he blows intense heat from his flared nostrils onto Rebecca's chest, neck and face, and Rebecca is saturated in sweat. Frustrated, she angrily removes her sweat-soaked nightclothes and throws them at the horse. "I'm not afraid of you, Menopause," Rebecca says.

Chapter 5

Everything Black

Naked, Rebecca wakes up on Tuesday morning but feels uncomfortable because she is drenched in sweat again.

"That bloody Menopause is irritating me. Ugh!" she grunts. She picks up her nightdress from the floor in the corner of the room and throws it in the linen basket. Hot, she goes to the bathroom, splashes her face with cold water, wets a small towel, and places it around her neck. She has a shower. She missed work yesterday because of her doctor's appointment and is determined to put on a good show today. She stares into her wardrobe and chooses a dark blouse, black trousers, and a long, black jacket. She has become one with her black jackets and wears them everywhere. She has a heavy-duty one for the winter, a mac for the spring and autumn, and one with a see-through, thin embroidered top, which is thicker at the bottom for the summer. Rebecca refuses to wear light-coloured clothes. She doesn't want to keep checking the bottom of her attire to see if there are any red patches. Nor does she want to be informed by a stranger of disaster. Heavens! She would be mortified.

Rebecca sighs as she looks at all the black and navy blue outfits in her wardrobe. She sucks her teeth as she moves one outfit to the side and then another. A voice in her head makes critical comments about her clothing, and she is not amused.

What's wrong with that woman, it says. *She always wears black like she is going to a funeral.*

At first, she disapproves of the critical comments, but then she agrees with their honesty. "Yes, you're right, Menopause. Black, black all the time," she says as she rummages through her wardrobe and flings some clothes over her head behind her.

Stepping over the clothes, Rebecca looks in the mirror. She touches her thinning hair and massages her face and neck. "My gosh! What happened to me? I've not looked properly in the mirror for what seems like an eternity, and I don't like what I see." She turns her back. "I've definitely had better days." Rebecca frowns as she prods several parts of her body. "I had not weighed myself for a while either and did not realise the weight was creeping on me," she says. She squeezes her lower abdomen and tucks the protruding fat back through the leg of her figure-flattering knickers. "This ain't flattering at all," she says, wincing.

Rebecca thinks about women her age she's seen on television who are fit and made up fabulously. "No wonder no one has looked at me for years. Not that I want another relationship, mind you. That would be impossible with my libido having lost its way, but it would be nice if someone at least glanced at me. I don't blame them, though." She wipes a tear that trickles down her saggy cheek.

She stares at the clock. "If only I could go back in time." She pulls at the "laugh lines" that were once attractive but now hang loose. As she curls back the corners of her lips, "It does not seem that long ago when people complimented me on the smoothness and firmness of my features," Rebecca says, remembering the days when the corners of her eyes would crinkle, not wrinkle when she smiled. Today, when she tries smiling and looks in the mirror, her eyes look squinty and sad instead of happy.

Moving away from the mirror, Rebecca reminds herself that she needs to go to work. "Anyway, I've got to get going. I love teaching the children and helping them achieve their goals," she declares. She rubs her face vigorously with coconut oil, paying attention to the "laugh lines" around her full lips and the wrinkles around the outside of her once beautiful hazel eyes.

Rebecca continues to rummage through the wardrobe as she chews her bottom lip. She is not pleased. "No, no, not this one," she says, flinging an array of long-forgotten clothes onto the bed. Pulling in her tummy and holding her breath, she tries on one outfit after the other but is unsatisfied. She turns her nose up at everything she touches. "Black, black, black, brown, dark blue, black," Rebecca says as she takes each garment off the hanger and throws it on the bed in frustration. She shifts her attention to some oldies but goodies. She tries them on, one by one, but nothing fits. "Too small, too small, too small. Bloody, too small."

How did that weight sneak up on me like that? she wonders. She jabs her tummy, slaps her thighs, and pinches her cheeks. Despondent, she sits on the bed, her head leaning on her shoulder in disgust. Her eyes beg the wardrobe for a miracle and rest on a floral top hanging above a pink pair of trousers. Pink platform shoes rest beneath them at the bottom of the wardrobe. She tries the shoes on, and they fit perfectly. "Yes!" She smiles, but that is short-lived because her arms refuse to go inside the sleeves of the floral top when she attempts to put it on. "Damn you!" she exclaims. In the arm/top war that follows, the top wins, and the arm is brutally defeated. She is also disappointed when her calf arrests the pink trouser leg and refuses to let it pass.

Rebecca kisses her teeth and sinks back into the bed in frustration. Closing her eyes with lips pressed together, her cheeks rise as she fondly remembers the good times at various nightclubs where she wore the tight pink trousers and that floral top, light and bright coloured clothing in the seventies and eighties, and how she turned heads. Rebecca pats her head as she ponders the creative art of crafting her well-groomed afro before leaving her home. She envisages herself standing near the walls and naming the clubs in her head; her cheeks rise even higher: *All Nations, Dougie's, Plashet, Rex, Little Eye, Red Lion, Room at the Top, Tiffany's, Palm Trees, Diamond* ... Her head drops in sadness into her cupped hands, and tears roll down her arms into the elbow creases, cascading down her tummy. "But they will never fit again," she says gloomily. "And my gorgeous hair. What happened to it?"

Cringing as she looks at her lower abdomen at a multitude of stretch marks laced across it, Rebecca sighs in disgust. Poking her tummy, she takes a deep breath and holds it, but there is no difference. "I can hardly see my bloody feet," Rebecca says in defeat. Rummaging through the drawers, amongst the many petite lingerie she hopes to wear again, she locates the girdle her mother-in-law gave her after her first baby. With furrowed brows and clenched lips, Rebecca remembers how annoyed she was because she had already returned to her pre-pregnant weight after having RD. *What the blooming hell is this?* she remembers thinking. Back then, Rebecca thought to throw the girdle out, but she had tossed it into the bottom drawer in disgust instead and forgot about it. Now, she's happy she kept it and tries it on again.

Unrolling the fabric, she attempts to pull the girdle over her thighs. No luck. Desperate, she lies on the bed, frowning and pulling, hoisting it over her figure-flattering knickers. She tucks in the excess abdominal flab, sticking out here and there. "I would love to wear my pink trousers and floral top with my pink shoes again. In fact, I would love to wear any light-coloured clothing, but until I conquer Menopause, it doesn't seem likely. Can you imagine all the bright clothes I have stored in a trunk, suitcases, and vacuum-packed bags under my bed that no longer fit? For now, it's always dark, bloody dark," she mutters. "Everything is dark."

Rebecca picks up the discarded garments and flings them to join the others on the side of the bed. Choosing something dreary from the wardrobe, unhappy Rebecca gets dressed. While she worries about what the future holds for her, her children, her grandson, grandchildren, and great-grandchildren who are not yet born, Menopause strikes again with a vengeance. Her skin burns, her head is hot, and her fresh clothes are wet with sweat. Rebecca pulls her clothes away from her body in anger. She wants to kick back, but she shouts instead. "Stop it, damn you! Why do you bother me like that?"

Naturally, Menopause doesn't listen.

"Give me a break! Will you!" Rebecca yells. She puts her fan on and clips her curly weave. "Look!" she points at her face. "Can't you see I've had enough?" She wipes her face with a towel.

The heat wave passes as if Menopause takes heed of her request. Rebecca changes her clothes yet again.

To compound matters, she is bleeding heavily and has to return to the bathroom. "What a mess," she moans.

Her throat is tight as she sits at the kitchen table and sips some cold water. "Good job, I got up early," she says. Her hands shake, and her breathing is erratic as she pours cereal into a bowl. Some flakes scatter on the table. She pours cold milk into the bowl. She would have loved to make cornmeal porridge, but that would make her even hotter. "When the bloody hell is this going to stop?" She pants.

Eventually, Rebecca manages to get ready for work. She places children's books she had taken home for marking, her planning folders, and some Tena Discreet Lady Extra Pads in her trolley and makes her way to work. With the fan blowing the highest it can go in the car, Rebecca sees herself in the mirror. She passes her finger around the sockets of her eyes. "I must get some sleep," she yawns.

Chapter 6

Cardigan on, Cardigan off

Feeling calmer, Rebecca is in her car on her way to work. Her thick black coat is on the seat beside her. She has taken the doctor's advice—exercising regularly, eating a balanced meal, taking some Menopace, and wearing thinner layers of clothing. She takes off one layer as she stops at the traffic light and opens her windows wider because she feels warm. She talks incessantly to herself and begs Menopause for relief.

"Why me? Why do you do this to me? How long will you continue harassing me? Why do you embarrass me like this?"

Again, Menopause does not answer.

Looking ahead, she observes a line of cars in front of her. There are eight, and behind her are many more. She looks at the time on her dashboard. It's half past seven. She has no choice but to wait, even though it will make her late.

"Why did I not leave home earlier?" she bellows,

looking at her distressed, sweaty face in the rear-view mirror.

Rebecca rechecks the dashboard. It's now minutes to eight o'clock. She stretches her neck to see if any cars in front of her have moved. They haven't. "What am I going to do? I know I won't get there on time," she wails.

The muscles in her face tense, and Rebecca can feel Menopause prancing due to her stress. The heat is moving from her neck to her face. Muttering, she fans herself with her hand and tries to open her window wider, but that's the widest it can go. She places her handheld fan towards her face, but that's no good. Frustrated, she twiddles her toes to relax the tense muscles in her legs. As she leans over, she accidentally places her foot on the accelerator instead of the brake. BANG!

"Oh, my gosh! What have I done?" Rebecca says, trying to hide her face from the ogling drivers. Her heart gallops. "I wasn't concentrating. That blooming Menopause! What's going to happen now?" She moves her head sideways to avoid the gaze of the angry person who is chattering and standing outside her car's passenger window with a wheel spanner in hand.

"What the bloody hell have you done? Did you not see my car in front of you?" the woman yells, attempting to open Rebecca's car door.

Rebecca holds her breath while the woman raises the spanner menacingly. Her eyes bulge out, and her nostrils flare. Armed with her anger at Menopause, Rebecca raises her head and exhales. She pushes the door open with her handbag in the air. The other woman's face softens as she observes the stream of sweat running down Rebecca's temples. Luckily, she's a parent of one of her pupils and changes her tone in recognition.

"Oh, Mrs Dawson, it's you? Are you okay, my dear?"

"Yes, yes. I'm so sorry. I was worried about being late for work and got brain fog. This menopause thing has really messed with my body and soul. It's playing a devastating game with me."

The other driver nods. "No problem, Mrs Dawson. The damage is minor, and I know where to find you. Oh, you said that you're suffering from brain fog. I heard through the grapevine that Frankincense oil helps many symptoms of menopause, especially brain fog and sleep problems. Maybe you should try it."

"Oh, yes. I am willing to try it if that helps. I will definitely consider that. Thank you, and sorry again."

"No problem. Good luck," the woman says, getting in her car and glancing back at Rebecca. "My time will come," she says aloud. "Later than sooner, I hope. I'm not ready for that."

Breathing a sigh of relief, Rebecca is grateful for an amicable outcome to a potentially volatile situation. When the damaged vehicle holding up traffic is removed from the road, the problem is resolved, and she drives on. She turns on the radio now that she feels much better because she has shared the burden of menopause with another woman who seemed sympathetic.

Stumbling on the Hibiscus-Rose Podcast 'Why Menopause' on the BBC, Rebecca listens with interest and nods as the women recount their harrowing experiences.

"The changes in my hormones played havoc in my mind and body—night sweats, anxiety, low self-esteem, and low self-confidence. I could not sleep. I walked around like a zombie. I thought I was going mad."

"I cried constantly. I did not know why. My husband did not understand what I was going through. He said I was irrational. He left me. HRT made me get my life back again."

"Good for you," Rebecca says.

"My head felt hot. It wanted to explode. I often trembled and tried to pull my hair out in anger. My body felt like it did not belong to me. It was like an out-of-body experience. I was not the same person. I had awful mood swings and did not know what to do. I had no desire for intimacy with my husband. He did not understand. I walked out. Angry and frustrated, I left my husband and went to live with my mum. She understood what I was going through. We've now reconciled. I shout about menopause."

"I hear you, Sis. Shout out as loud as you can!"

Rebecca roars.

"I went through early menopause at the age of twenty-four because my ovaries stopped making the expected levels of hormones. I was devastated. It wasn't easy because HRT was not readily available on the NHS then. It was a difficult and emotional experience. Thankfully, I was prescribed HRT. Shout about HRT. Shout about early menopause."

"I am shouting for you," Rebecca yells.

"I felt so unwell during the menopause, so I started to take more time off work. My boss was not sympathetic to my predicament. I lost my job."

"Damn them!" Rebecca yells.

"Menopause tormented me. It made me depressed and very anxious. I found it difficult to go to work, go out, or meet friends. Fortunately, my doctor prescribed anti-depressants. My family, my friends, my boss and my colleagues were supportive. I am still at work, and I am getting there."

"Good for you! Good for them!" Rebecca shouts. "Wishing you all the best, love."

"When I went through the "change", I had no problems, but my mate went through 'ell. She had to see a psychiatrist, poor thing. She is okay now."

"Thank God." Rebecca says empathetically. "I'm so glad she is ok." Rebecca hopes she does not go through what the woman's friend went through."

"I felt the force of menopause after I had a total hysterectomy because of fibroids. My womb, ovaries and cervix were removed. They left me with nothing. I was emotional. My life was unbearable. I made my family's life unbearable. I was not expecting that."

"I feel brutalised, embarrassed, and ashamed because of an imbalance in my hormones. They call them oestrogen, progesterone, and testosterone. All three are a mystery to me!"

Banging on the dashboard, Rebecca says, "That's right! Brutal, aren't they those hormones? So embarrassing! Menopause embarrasses you in private and in public! My sentiments precisely! Shout about menopause!"

Rebecca takes ownership of her common situation by sympathising with the women going through the same thing. She is grateful to the partners, carers, and young adults who have bravely shared their experiences about the impact menopause has on families, friends, and themselves. She praises the husband, who said it was a challenging experience when his wife was going through menopause. He was grateful that he stayed with his wife and supported her to get her life again. "Good on you!" Rebecca tells them as if they can hear her. With conviction, Rebecca bids them to continue supporting their loved ones and encourages them to ask for help. "Shout about menopause!" she cries, even though she knows no one can hear her.

Rebecca is encouraged by what she has heard on the podcast. The knowledge and experience shared reinforce what she read in Dr Lily's pamphlets. Feeling enlightened, she diagnoses herself as perimenopausal. "Aha! I am simply flirting with menopause while transitioning naturally," she says. Rebecca sings along with "Roar", a song by Katy Perry on the radio. "I'm taking the horse by the reins. You held me down, but I got up …"

Righto. I will tame Menopause and face it head-on, she thinks. *I will take the reins and ride like the wind. Menopause, I am going to shout about you to whoever will listen. You've held me down for far too long!*

Rebecca waits a short while in the school car park before exiting her vehicle. She takes some under-eye cream from her bag and applies it to the dark areas around her eyes. Then she brushes her hair and clips it in a bun.

As she leaves the car, a young lady walks up to Rebecca and compliments her on her attire. "You sure look great this morning, Mrs Dawson," she says, smiling. "Your green necklace and matching earrings, as well as the beautiful beads and jewels on your black top, complement your eyes."

Rebecca dimly wonders who this young lady is. "Thank you, my dear," she says as they walk in the same direction.

Looking at the beautiful reception play area behind the corrugated fence, Rebecca smiles.

*

Upon arrival at the front school gate, Rebecca confidently lifts her chest. Her clear hazel eyes survey the newly built school building. Clasping her hands in prayer, she is thankful to be working in such an educationally sound institution, so different from the previous school where she taught. This school serves a multicultural population, and people work together for the betterment of the school community. She likes that and is proud to spend six to eight hours in this place where teachers, children, parents, and staff work together to encourage children to reach their full potential.

Rebecca gazes at heaven, praying for strength to cope with her day. Then she pulls her trolley and aims for the building, putting her best foot forward.

She acknowledges everyone she passes—from the office staff to cleaners, cooks, teaching staff, dinner staff, voluntary staff, parents, the site and senior managers. She enters her classroom enthusiastically even though she feels exhausted and menstruates heavily. As she prepares for her day's work, she makes sure her bladder is empty, and her clothing is not stained with blood. Sitting on the toilet, she clasps her hands again in devotional prayer.

"Thank you, Almighty, for enabling me to be the best mother, grandmother, daughter, friend, teacher, colleague and community worker I can be. I acknowledge your presence in all I do. Grant me patience, resilience, and determination to carry on.

And please, please God, give me some relief from that rascal Menopause."

It is 8:40, and Rebecca goes to the playground to collect her pupils as they arrive. Parents greet her, and so do her Year 2 students. Six to seven-year-old children are inquisitive, love the interactive, fun, and engaging way Rebecca teaches, and look forward to attending school every day. The young lady Rebecca greeted in the car park earlier introduces herself as Daisy, Rebecca's mentee. Rebecca forgot she would be starting her placement today but welcomes her warmly.

Rebecca scrunches her hankie in the palm of her sweaty hand. Daisy observes her mentor as each child shakes Rebecca's hand and walks into the classroom in an orderly manner. They undertake their tasks independently, and Daisy is impressed. When she sits in on a phonics lesson Rebecca teaches, she admires how the children approach the task with excitement and a passion for learning. She also admires the way they are learning to read and write with such obvious enjoyment.

Daisy wonders how Rebecca manages to control each child's behaviour so effectively, but as she observes her mentor's calm and positive approach to each individual, she understands.

She loves her mentor's animated voice when teaching and tries to emulate her but realises it will take practice.

It takes a special skill to do what my mentor does so well. She seems to love her job and does it selflessly, Daisy thinks. *I want to be a teacher like Mrs Dawson, but I have so much to learn.*

When a pupil tells Rebecca there's water on her face, Rebecca laughs. "Thank you for noticing, my dear," she acknowledges as she wipes the sweat with her hankie. Daisy also noticed the perspiration but didn't want to embarrass her revered mentor. She wonders whether she will have the same experience in the future, but she doesn't want to think about this right now.

It is planning and preparation time, so Rebecca does not teach that afternoon. She needs time to plan and prepare her dynamic lessons. Even though her top is wet with perspiration, Rebecca focuses on the tasks. She gets up a few times to go to the toilet with a sanitary pack in her bag and then returns to her computer desk. She takes off her cardigan, puts it back on again, and does it so repetitively that Menopause wants to take remedial action. Sweating, Rebecca goes to the toilet again, takes off her damp top, and tries to dry it under the hand drier.

She hopes Menopause will be sympathetic and give her a break while indisposed, but he gives her a lashing instead. Her head is on fire, her skin burns, and her underarms are soaked.

When Daisy enters the toilet, Rebecca pulls on her top like nothing has happened. Back at her desk, she stands to retrieve a document, but she doesn't see the wet red patch on the chair on which she is sitting. However, a female colleague spots the embarrassment and is too uncomfortable to tell Rebecca, so she waits for her reaction.

Rebecca looks at the seat and then at her colleague but doesn't say anything. She drags the chair to a distant corner of the room and turns it around. Taking a damp cloth from the sink, Rebecca dips it in soapy water and cleans the seat briskly. She takes the cloth to the toilet and solemnly puts it in a bin. Luckily, Rebecca is wearing dark clothing, allowing her to maintain some dignity. She returns to her classroom to retrieve the spare clothing she keeps in the cupboard and freshens up in the bathroom. As she walks back into the room, her colleague's eyes follow her. Rebecca shrugs her shoulders, picks up her things, and waves goodbye.

Chapter 7

Where has Rebecca gone?

Returning home from work, Rebecca puts her trolley aside and flops into her chair. With her head perched in her hands, she SIGHS! She tries to unwind, but the vision of her colleague staring at her as she stood beside the chair disturbs her. Remembering the woman's advice earlier, she purchases Frankincense essential oil from Amazon Prime, hoping to receive it the next day. Rebecca is despondent as she reflects on what happened during the day. Not only is she a disaster in the kitchen at home and driving her car, but now she might probably be the brunt of cruel jokes by a few of her colleagues at work. Standing and looking in the mirror, Rebecca wonders where young, strong Rebecca has gone. She questions why the reflection in the mirror barely resembles that missing person.

Pushing deliberately at the skin near her temple back, Rebecca shakes her head in dismay. She thinks about her time at university, her children, and her failed marriage.

"Where has the time gone?" She follows the lines of her eyebrows with her index fingers and pulls back the wrinkles on the sides of her eyes. She tugs at the short hairs under her chin and tries to pluck them out, but they are defiant and refuse to move. She battles on. When unsuccessful, she digs her nails into her skin and pulls until blood seeps. Exhaling, Rebecca lifts her weave to expose her hidden grey hairs and her sweaty, receding hairline. "Where has Rebecca gone?" she asks the heartless mirror as she walks away.

She takes a shower and puts on her black jogging bottoms and a grey shirt. She goes into the kitchen and stares at the fridge as if in a daze because she has forgotten why she is there. Trying to wrack her brain, she doesn't remember the reason. "Bloody brain fog," she swears, opening and closing several cupboards. Most of them are left standing wide open while she returns to the fridge, pulls a face, and scratches her head, only to return to the cupboard again.

"Am I crazy? What the bloody hell is happening to me?" she asks.

An older friend has advised her that when and where she experiences these brain fog moments, she should stand still, wait until it clears, and remember what she's doing. But her friend did not specify how long, so Rebecca waits patiently but to no avail. Eventually, she opens the freezer and finds her lost hairbrush. "Oh, damn!" she shouts. "Am I going out of my mind?"

Shantel and her brother RD hear their mother cursing in the adjacent room.

"What's going on with Mum? I'm really worried," RD tells his sister.

"It's that menopause problem she was speaking about the other day. You know …"

Although Shantel can talk to her brother about many things, she feels uncomfortable discussing their mum's change of life experience.

RD looks at his sister and pinches his cleft chin. "Hmm. I remember that day vividly. I wanted to bury my head in the sofa cushion, Sis, or put my fingers in my ears when she talked about the woman thing."

Shantel pulls a face. "Woman thing? Ha! I heard that men suffer from menopause, too."

"Men? Nah. Pause, Sis. Can't imagine me sitting in front of a fan all day to keep the heat away."

His sister smiles. "Give it up, RD. *Men-Oh-Pause*. Get it? Menopause." She knows menopause is when a woman's menstrual cycle stops. Still, it is not confirmed until twelve months after the period stops. Shantel also knows that most women will experience menopause between 45 and 55 and last between seven and fourteen years. Perimenopause is the natural transition time around menopause before the period stops. During this time, many women, not all, experience many uncomfortable and distressing symptoms. She knows that her mother started experiencing menopausal symptoms months earlier, a common trait for black women, and also, her mother's menopausal symptoms might last longer than women from other cultures and be more severe. Still, she doesn't discuss this with her brother. However, Shantel feels sorry for her mother because she is troubled by menopause, and Shantel is concerned that she might soon start experiencing the same symptoms herself. *Eek! Perish the thought.* She does not want to consider that right now. "RD, you need to find out about menopause because when you find the lady of yours, you will be able to help her to cope should she have those awful symptoms."

"But I thought we were talking about Mum," RD says, trying to deflect the focus from him.

"We are. Mum said she has had enough of her dry skin, tiredness, sleeplessness, mood swings, and lack of concentration. But worst of all are the sweats and brain fog."

He nods sympathetically.

"RD, I'm concerned about how irritable Mum has become. I can't even ask a simple question or make a statement without her reacting irrationally. Your mother, Rebecca, is a lovely, intelligent woman. Still, sometimes, I find it difficult to live with her because of her constant scrutiny, negativity, and unpredictability. I'm tired of checking her face before I even say good morning. If it's scowling, I know I've got to stay away."

RD sighs. "And our mum burns our favourite meals," he says, pouting.

"Bruv, it's difficult times at home. Sometimes, I just want to pack my things and find somewhere else to live. I can afford to do that, but I love our mum and want to be near her."

"I hear you, Sis."

Shantel perches her forehead on her fingers in worry. "Poor Mummy. We must continue to be caring and patient even if she's irrational."

"Mummy?"

"Okay, that's taking it too far. Let's call Rebecca Mum. But if she's not complaining about hot flushes and heavy periods, it's something else. Remember how she used to love wearing vibrant, psychedelic colours? But the dull, drab clothes she wears now are so drab and boring."

RD chuckles. "Dressing in black seems to be in fashion on the estate, but no one's told Tyrell."

"You mean that irritating friend of yours?"

"That's him. You know how he likes wearing all those bright colours? Well, one day, dressed in his yellow suit, yellow beret, and a multi-coloured tie, he saw Mum wearing all black and asked whether she was going to a funeral!"

"A funeral? No more funerals, I hope," Shantel says with fear in her eyes. "Too many young people are killing each other these days. Why do they have no love for each other? Without love, there is no respect, and without respect, there is no love. No more killing. No more funerals."

"You sound just like Mum. She cares about the young people. She cares about others. She needs to learn to care about herself, too. If you ask me, Mum deffo needs to wear brighter colours," RD says. "That's precisely what the community's young people should do. Shantel, we need to get Mum involved in community work again."

"Right. And we also need to help Mum cope with this menopause issue. Mum went to see her doctor on Monday, and she has another appointment next week. I hope she will find it easy to negotiate the healthcare system and get the care she is entitled to and deserves."

"Mum is a soldier. I'm sure she will."

"Mum has a lovely doctor who cares about people, so she will be okay. But I think she is lonely and needs a companion. RD, we need to find her a man. I'm not saying that is the solution to menopause, but this might help stop her loneliness and isolation. Our young people are undoubtedly our future, but our mum needs a future, too."

"Deffo!" he says, flicking his fingers. "When we put the next march to address the pressing issue of gun and knife crimes in the community, I will be taking over Mum's chairperson role because she says she finds it difficult to concentrate and cannot give her best right now. Of course, I'll try my best to ensure that young people are properly informed so they can make good choices, but I wish Mum was there with me. People love and respect her, and she will be missed."

Shantel nods. "Hopefully, our mother can talk to her doctor about her problems and find out what can be done. I would encourage every woman to do the same. If they cannot talk to a doctor, I urge them to talk to someone else. Hope our mum can find a solution to her problems."

"Agree," RD gives her a high five. "Under all that grumpiness, Mum is still an angel."

"Yes, Bro. She's an angel who needs someone to look out for her now."

Meanwhile, Rebecca adds a few drops of Frankincense to her diffuser. She stands beside it and conducts the breathing technique Dr Lily taught her. Rebecca hoped to feel an immediate calm. But, unhappy and disappointed she is not getting the direct benefit, she turns the diffuser off in frustration. Rebecca SIGHS! As she sits on her feet tucked underneath her on the sofa in the corner of the barely lit room, she intertwines her fingers and pats her index fingers on her lips. Reflective, she considers the Health and Wellbeing sessions offered at work. *What did Althea say in that session?* she thinks. She looks to the sky as if tracing for an answer from above. She stops. "Aha!"

"They will engage and inspire you, and furthermore, they will improve your mental health and physical well-being, enable you to develop trusting relationships and help you to thrive and achieve your potential. Menopause is affected by stress, and the Well-being group can also help you address this."

So, Rebecca decides it will be good for her. "I won't lose anything by going, so I might as well. I will attend the Calming, Mindfulness and Meditation workshops and the Laughter and Happiness sessions. I've been evading them for far too long. These will do me good."

Chapter 8

Buying Time

Shantel is committed to spending quality time with her mum. Their lives have been overtaken by work and caring for Phoenix, and they have less time to spend together.

But today, Phoenix is with his dad, Silk, and RD is out with the lads, hoping to find the lady who will make a difference in his life. So, this is mum and daughter time, and they intend to enjoy it.

Rebecca puts some Frankincense oil in the diffuser. She sits with her feet flat on the floor with her knees slightly lower than her hips. Shantel sits beside her, adopting the same position. Rebecca breathes in deeply, and Shantel copies. She breathes out, and Shantel does the same. They develop a mother-daughter rhythmic breathing pattern, and they both laugh. Calmly, Rebecca stands as she and her daughter converse about life. While Rebecca crushes the garlic and cuts up an onion and bell pepper, she blinks excessively, her face twitches and her hands move involuntarily as she watches Shantel dice pieces of pumpkin with a sharp knife and put them in a Dutch pot of water to boil. She says, "Shantel, be careful! Mind that knife. Cut it like this." She demonstrates. As Shantel puts the dumplings, carrots, green bananas, yams, dasheen and celery in the pot, Rebecca warns her. "Don't put them in like that. You'll burn yourself."

Her daughter finds this annoying, but she says nothing. She doesn't want to spoil their "home alone" time together, especially as she knows her mum continues to be tortured with the symptoms of menopause.

Rebecca adds a small amount of salt, thyme, and her special seasoning to the mixture. She is about to toss in a scotch bonnet pepper but remembers what Dr Lily said about spicy foods. Taking a deep breath to capture the aroma of their alluring soup and breathing out slowly, they are contented that they have done an excellent job. They high-five each other.

"Well done, Rebecca," Shantel says.

"No, well done, Miss Shantel," her mother responds, hugging her daughter. They both laugh, leave the soup to simmer, and sit talking about the past. Although some of the conversations are painful, they support each other in the decision to remove Blake from their lives. Rebecca suddenly jumps off her seat as if she is about to sprint. She rushes towards the window and opens it wide. She waits for menopause to taunt her, but he passes by, leaving a little heat behind.

Lovingly, Shantel fans her mum, who is yet again sweating. She then puts a shawl over her mother's shoulders as she overcomes the hot flush. Shantel lies on the sofa with her head on her mum's lap.

As they talk about Mrs Campbell, the mother of Shantel's deceased friend Raven, Shantel sits up. Her eyes are filled with tears as she thinks about her friend.

Rebecca comforts her, and they hug each other, never wanting to let go of Raven's memory. Drying her tears, Shantel leads her mum to the table and dishes two bowls of hearty pumpkin soup.

"This smells delicious, darling," Rebecca says. "Mmmm."

She wipes her sweaty forehead as she tucks in. Blowing the soup on the spoon to cool it, Rebecca says, "I feel so sorry for Raven's parents. Can they ever come to terms with her violent death?" She sighs. "I don't think we have done enough to support them. But I'll have more time to visit now that RD has taken over the running of the community group."

Shantel puts down her spoon. "Me too. I feel sorry for Miss Elsie and Mr Walter," she says, "Yes. We must revisit them. The thing about supporting people who have lost someone is that it needs to be consistent. Some people prefer to be on their own whilst grieving; others want company because they get lonely and need someone to talk to, someone who will listen. Many of us make promises, but we don't fulfil them, but things happen. Life happens. It is what it is."

Rebecca jumps up to open the window wider and then resumes her seat at the table. "Sorry," she says, "I'm listening."

"Anyway, we must make every effort to stop by if that's what they want," Shantel says, leaning across the table and wiping the sweat from her mother's forehead with her napkin.

*

"Where has the time gone?" Rebecca asks the stranger, who is staring back at her in the mirror. It is now two weeks since she attended her first doctor's appointment. She was meant to return for a follow-up last week, but she'd forgotten. She's annoyed with herself and wonders whether she will be given another chance. Full of apologies, Rebecca calls the doctor's surgery for another appointment.

"Okay, Mrs Dawson, but can you please ring if you cannot attend your appointment, as we'll need to allocate it to someone else," the receptionist informs her.

"Sorry, I forgot," she explains. "I had more episodes of brain fog."

"Alright, Mrs Dawson," the receptionist says.

She gives Rebecca a time and date for her next visit. "Needless to say, it is of uttermost importance that you attend your next appointment. I suggest you leave a note where you can easily see the appointment date—maybe on the fridge or the reminder on your phone. Again, it is important for you to attend."

"Yes, yes. I will attend."

"Alright, Dr Lily will see you then."

As soon as they hang up, Rebecca leaves a note near her wardrobe and another on the bookcase in her bedroom. She loves reading, and it would be impossible to miss it there.

Meanwhile, Rebecca continues to be tormented by Menopause. He has attacked her, set her on fire, and drenched her. He's kept her awake and given her painful knees from so much praying. Just now, she wakes up with her heart beating at speed, and there are beads of sweat on her forehead. She sits up, holding her chest, thinking she is having a heart attack. Panic-stricken, she dials 999.

Breathless, she says, "I think I'm having a heart attack."

"Okay, take a deep breath and tell me what is happening," the operator says. "Have you got chest pain?"

"No, but my heart is beating extremely fast."

"Palpitations, okay," she says.

She asks a set of questions, but Rebecca's breathing and heart rate have returned to normal by the time she has completed her drill. Sheepishly, Rebecca says she's feeling better now. "It's that damn menopause," she whimpers.

"I understand," says the operator. "Sorry."

"No, I'm sorry," says Rebecca. "I shouldn't have bothered you. I know how busy you are."

Soaked in sweat, Rebecca gets off the bed to change her nightie and the bedding. She fetches a glass of water and guzzles it down. Still thirsty, she fills the glass again and sits on the bed, sipping thoughtfully.

Yawning, Rebecca arrives at work early the following day despite having no sleep. "Ahhh-hhaaa! No sleep at all," she mumbles, walking down the school corridor. She is one of the first teaching staff there, and apart from the office staff and the site supervisors, Rebecca sees no one else on the route. Yawning, she sits with the window wide open, contemplating what is happening to her and what she should do about it. Although she is annoyed with the viciousness of menopause, Rebecca has been taking Menopace. She stubbornly dismisses the urgency to attend her appointment to see Dr Lily. "I'm sure I will get over this soon," Rebecca repeats like a prayer. But then she decides she must attend just in case.

Rebecca is distracted from her thoughts as Daisy enters the cold classroom. She is surprised to see her mentor wearing a thin top. "Good morning, Mrs Dawson. How are you? Aren't you cold? It's quite chilly in here," Daisy says, shivering.

In preparing a comfortable environment for her pupils, Rebecca closes the window. "Didn't realise that it was so cold. The cold means nothing at my age and stage," she replies. "But we definitely want the classroom to be warm for when the pupils arrive."

Daisy changes her focus to that day's lesson.

They discuss effective strategies for Daisy to teach the pupils and how she will successfully implement them. Rebecca praises her for being such a resolute trainee, and Daisy smiles from ear to ear. She enjoys being mentored by Rebecca and is developing good teaching skills by emulating her style.

But today, Daisy is concerned. She has noticed that Rebecca seems irritated with her and her colleagues. She's still tolerant of the children but is easily distracted and often loses concentration. Daisy watches Rebecca as she scribes on the whiteboard, composing a story with the children, but her pen is stuck on the word "the".

She pauses for a moment, avoiding Daisy's gaze. She cannot understand what's happening but tries to disguise the turbulence she feels inside by reading out loud with the pupils. Daisy is impressed by Rebecca's exaggeration, intonation, and animation but is worried about the lapse in the lesson. Leaving the classroom to go home, Rebecca walks in a busy corridor, mumbling about her recurring brain fog.

Chapter 9
No Sleep at All

As soon as she gets home, Rebecca has a shower. Worried about her lack of concentration and possible memory loss, she puts some Frankincense in the diffuser. Taking deep breaths, she waits for the essential oil to take effect. Rebecca falls asleep but wakes up at eight o'clock that evening. "Oh, dear," she says, "I fell asleep. How am I going to sleep tonight?" Making a light meal, Rebecca reflects on her experience at work and is not at all pleased. With her ego bruised, she struggles to eat dinner as she wonders what her trainee thinks. "I must make sure that does not happen again. I've got too much to lose—my pride, dignity, and reputation." She grapples with the idea of discussing her struggles with the headteacher who is understanding. Still, she wonders whether it will be assumed that she is incapable or inadequate. So, instead, she decides to attend the Health and Wellbeing sessions for staff at work to boost her morale, help her unwind and find strategies to help her cope with her stressful life. "It will be good for my mental health," she says.

Rebecca watches television to distract her thoughts but gets bored after a while. Taking Dr Lily's advice for dealing with brain fog, she engages in her puzzle activity. Yawning after hours of the activity, Rebecca sprays her pillow with Frankincense and exhausted from work, she is fast asleep within no time.

It is the night before her next doctor's appointment. Rebecca feels as if she's being crushed by Menopause. She wakes up in a panic. With hot flushes raging, she cannot sleep, so she walks around the room with her eyes wide open. Attempting to go back to sleep, her eyes refuse to close. The mirror entices her to engage in its demand. "Look at me, woman," it tells her. Rebecca looks in the mirror and is frightened by the woman staring at her. She covers her face with her hand.

Burning hot, Rebecca wants to run out of the house naked into the cold to cool her body and head, but seconds later, she's cold and puts a blanket around her. She paces from one room to another—from the sitting room into the kitchen, from the kitchen into her bedroom, and back into the sitting room. Roaming up and down the stairs, scratching and rubbing her arms, neck, and face, exhausted, Rebecca sits down in her armchair.

Her heartbeat quickens, and her breathing is fast. She lifts her hair off her forehead and wipes the sweat with a flannel. Wanting to pull the weave off her head and fling it in the corner, she decides it's not a good idea because she doesn't want to lose any more of her natural hair. Rebecca taps her head with her fingers to distract the unwelcoming thoughts. Her fear deepens as she thinks she is "going mad".

Rebecca bursts into tears. She sits in her dark room, places a wet flannel over her eyes and eventually falls asleep. Minutes later, she awakes and flings the flannel across the room. "Bloody Menopause!" she yells. "Stop it! You're so damn annoying." Menopause lashes her for the insult, and Rebecca is distressed.

The commotion wakes Shantel. Rubbing her eyes, she runs into her mother's room.

"What's going on, Mum? What's wrong with you?"

Her arms move in every direction. "Menopause is attacking me again," Rebecca cries.

"Attacking you? Menopause? What do you mean, Mum? Who is attacking you?" Shantel asks, concerned.

"He won't stop."

"He?" Shantel looks around the room. She searches under the bed and in and behind the wardrobe. She lifts the curtain but cannot see anyone. "Mum, what are you saying?

Her mum sobs louder. "He's ruining my life, that horse Menopause. I can't take it anymore."

Shantel is concerned. "Mum, we need to do something, and fast." Shantel hugs her mum and takes her to bed. She pats her Mum's shoulder and sweat-soaked hair and tells her it will be alright. Rebecca eventually falls asleep to Shantel's reassuring words and comforting embrace.

Frightened by what happened the previous night and the implications of what might happen, Rebecca realises the gravity of the situation. She decides she must keep her upcoming appointment with Dr Lily. She hates to miss work again, but she has no choice. The way she feels right now, Rebecca cannot face anyone except Dr Lily. She arrives early for her appointment, desperate for help.

Rebecca wears sunglasses to hide the bags under her wide-open eyes. This reminds her of when she wore sunglasses to hide her shame and avoid recognition when RD was in prison. She walks into the GP practice, acknowledging the receptionist. Although worried, she is calmer this time. She waits patiently to be seen.

"Mrs Dawson. I'm glad you could keep your appointment today," Dr Lily tells Rebecca.

"I'm back again, Dr Lily. Can't take it anymore. I'm sorry I wasn't able to attend last time. Honestly, I forgot."

"It's okay. You're here now. Can you tell me how you feel and what's happening?"

"Well, I've certainly not been feeling myself lately. I feel zombified. My eyes refuse to close. See?" She removes her sunglasses and squeezes her eyes together, but they spring open again.

"Okay, that's weird. But you said you're not feeling yourself? Can you explain what you mean?"

"I feel like a different person."

"A different person?"

Rebecca covers her eyes with tears threatening. "Yes. I look in the mirror and don't see myself. I do not see Rebecca. I don't know the woman sitting here in front of you." She looks at Dr Lily and shakes her head.

"Can you explain a bit more?"

Rebecca looks at Dr Lily and then looks down at the table as she explains how she feels. She avoids eye contact. "Well, I used to be confident and independent. I did everything by myself, but now I feel like I'm starting to depend on others, and I don't like that. I'm losing my confidence. I get anxious and irritable easily with adults … but I'm still okay with children."

Rebecca sighs. "Sometimes, I feel overwhelmed and cannot understand why. I cry for no reason. And it's so difficult for me to sleep. Do you think I'm depressed? Can I have something for that? My friends said I should ask you."

"I'm glad you've asked, but I would like to find out some more information before we consider that."

"Okay, Dr Lily. When I close my eyes, it's like I'm watching a film—certainly not enjoyable. I sweat a lot and have to change my clothing all the time. It's a lot of washing. Here's a list of the other things I've not yet told you about."

Dr Lily inspects the beads of sweat on Rebecca's face as she accepts the list and reads it out loud. "Cannot Sleep, Frustrated, Anxious, Mood Swings, Extremely Tired, Cannot Concentrate, Brain Fog, Dry Skin, Dry Vagina …" Her eyes follow as Rebecca stands unexpectedly and rushes towards the window. Dr Lily observes the perspiration dripping off Rebecca's nose. "I am sorry you're going through so much," Dr Lily says.

"You're sorry? Then how can you help me?" Rebecca asks. The urgency in her voice is evident. "The over-the-counter pills aren't working. Menopace still hasn't given me relief. I am hot, bothered, itchy, frustrated and anxious, and now I have headaches. One minute, I'm happy, and the next, I'm sad. My heart gallops like …"

"A wild horse?"

"That's right. How do you know that?"

"Many women suffering from menopause compare their symptoms to that of a wild horse, in that their unwanted behaviour is annoying, repetitive, purposeful, frustrating and time-consuming."

"Sounds like Menopause in my dream. It is bloody frustrating. Sorry, Doctor Lily. Excuse my language. Its breath and hooves are hot, and it drenches me. I have to change my clothing and bed linen several times. It is time-consuming. I have to put on and take off my cardigan repeatedly. It also charges at me, making my heart beat fast, and it kicks me to wake me up because it does not want me to sleep. I am exhausted. That wretch bites me, too." Rebecca scratches her face, shoulder, back and thighs and rubs her arm.

"Yes, those dreams can be frustrating. Many women compare their fast heart speed to the galloping of a wild horse. I'm sorry the symptoms of menopause are still bothering you."

Rebecca fans herself repetitively. She puts the fan down and scratches and rubs her arm repeatedly. She fans herself again. "I have taken Menopace religiously to get rid of these annoying symptoms, but it is not working. How can you help me?" Rebecca puffs.

"Would you like me to put this fan on?" Dr Lily asks.

"Please do. Thank you. How can you help me, Dr Lily?"

"You said you take the Menopace regularly. Is that every day?"

"Well, as often as I can. I sometimes forget."

"It must be taken daily Mrs Dawson, so you can feel the full benefits."

Fanning herself continually, Rebecca wipes the sweat staining her underarms and presses her upper arms closer to her body. "I knew I should have worn a black top." She sits closer to the fan, her face etched with embarrassment. "My heart is beating extremely fast right now, like that of a galloping wild horse," Rebecca says, taking deep breaths and letting them out slowly.

Dr Lily checks Rebecca's pulse, waits a short while and rechecks it. She takes Rebecca's blood pressure. "You've coped very well with the hot flush, Mrs Dawson. Your blood pressure is fine."

"Well, like I told you on the phone …" Rebecca pauses for a short while. "Hmm. I can't remember, but that's it! My memory loss! Do you see what I mean?"

Dr Lily nods. "Yes, I can see that. Are you still exercising regularly, eating well-balanced meals, and meditating? Have you started playing chess yet?"

"I do all those things, but I guess I need to put more effort into doing these and being consistent," Rebecca smiles. "I find it difficult to concentrate, so chess is challenging, but I will keep at it. I like it. That Queen can move anywhere she wants. Isn't that great? I enjoy doing puzzles, too, and I do this at every opportunity. Sometimes, it takes a long time, but I persevere. Maybe I should take the Menopace for a bit longer. I don't think I've given it enough time."

"What you say is advisable, Mrs Dawson. Sometimes, it takes a bit longer to feel the benefit. I suggest you record when you have taken it."

Rebecca takes a see-through container from her big bag. "Dr Lily, I've also started blending and drinking brightly coloured blended vegetables and fruits. Look." She shows Dr Lily her drink. "Yum." Rebecca's face says it all.

"That's great! Because those blended drinks can keep you going for the day—an energy booster. It contains vitamins, proteins, fibre-rich carbohydrates, minerals, fibre and antioxidants; and healthy fats for good physical and mental health. Here is some information about the benefits of vegetable and fruit smoothies. You can get more information online. Do you want these?"

"Yes, please!"

I love your enthusiasm, determination and perseverance, Mrs Dawson."

"Thanks, and oh, here's the diary of my periods."

Dr Lily scrutinises the diary. "This looks fine," she reassures Rebecca.

Rebecca and her doctor discuss the possibility that she's going through perimenopause. *Exactly what I thought,* Rebecca internalises. Rebecca nods, but as the doctor is about to examine her, she holds her breath.

"Relax," Dr Lily advises as she examines her, encouraging Rebecca to take deep, controlled breaths. "I've not yet received the blood result." Dr Lily says and checks her computer. She shakes her head. "I haven't received it yet."

"That's not professional," Rebecca says. She was hoping to find the result of her blood test today.

"Unfortunately, that happens sometimes. I'm sorry. I will take more blood for a full blood count to check your hormone levels, Vitamin D and Vitamin B12 levels, and to check if there are problems with your thyroid glands."

"Thyroid gland?"

Dr Lily nods. "The thyroid is a small butterfly-shaped gland in your neck that produces hormones that help transform food we eat into energy. There can be similar symptoms to menopause if there are problems with the thyroid gland—like mood swings and anxiety, for example."

Rebecca touches her neck and opens her mouth wide. "Ho-hum! I'm so tired. I need your help, Dr Lily. I was about to ask you again about prescribing antidepressants for my anxiety, lack of sleep and mood swings. I know a few people whose doctors have prescribed it for those symptoms, but now I see why we must get it right. Yes, we must explore other possibilities first. Thank you." She yawns again.

"Yes. We might have to consider antidepressants or HRT, but we must wait for the blood test result.'

"What did you say about Vitamin B12?"

"I haven't said anything yet. Well, you might also have some symptoms of menopause if there is a lack of Vitamin B12 in your body, like extreme tiredness, headaches and noticeable heartbeat- palpitations. So, it is important we check that. But in the meantime, as advised earlier, wear layers of cotton clothing so it will be easier to take some off when your body feels hot and uncomfortable. Keep your room cool and use cotton bedding. You need to continue your exercise regime with which you are comfortable and eat a healthy diet. Practising meditation is beneficial, too."

"I have started attending the Wellbeing sessions at work, so I've learnt to meditate more effectively now and to laugh out loud without embarrassment. Laughter is the best medicine." Rebecca laughs loudly, and at first, Dr Lily looks at her concerned. Rebecca continues laughing, and Dr Lily laughs.

"That's the way to do it," Rebecca laughs. Dr Lily laughs.

Rebecca wipes her tears of laughter. "Doctor Lily, do you recommend essential oils as an alternative treatment for menopause symptoms?"

"We do not because there isn't enough research to suggest how useful they are, but some patients have told me that since using Frankincense oils, they sleep better, they are calmer, they sweat less, and their memory has improved."

Rebecca smiles with hope. Feeling comfortable after her laughing session, Rebecca says, "I have started using Frankincense oil but will persevere and let you know if there are benefits. Oh, I've started to use oestrogen cream down below." Rebecca smirks. "I will persist." Rebecca winks, and Dr Lily smiles.

"Okay. I will call you to let you know the result as soon as they come back and what we will do next."

Rebecca says thank you and leaves feeling calm and hopeful.

Chapter 10
Forgive Yourself

Rebecca comes home from work early the next day. Her shoulders are rounded. Exhausted, she falls asleep on her bed, fully clothed. Debilitating thoughts attack her head as the voice of her ex-husband, Blake, beats on her ear drum.

I used to be like you, a mere weakling.

Rebecca cries out in her mind but physically remains silent.

Look at you, crying again.

Rebecca covers her head with her pillow but still has no strength to challenge him.

Blake points at her. *You had all the power. You told me what to do, what to eat and how to behave. Nothing I did was right. Now, look at you. Ha! I am stronger than you now.*

Rebecca wakes from her sleep panting. But now that her ex-husband has finished abusing her, Menopause takes over by snorting fire from his nostrils into her head. She places the cool flannel on her forehead, but the heat overwhelms her. In distress, Rebecca puts some Frankincense oil on her fingers and gently rubs it on her temples. She sniffs it. Rebecca calls Mr Xavier. She has not done so for a while because she's been trying to cope on her own. Fortunately, they have agreed that when Rebecca needs to talk, she can call him anytime.

"I've called you, Mr Xavier, because I have been having these awful dreams about my son and ex-husband and now about Menopause."

"Okay. Would you like to talk about this?"

"Of course. That's one of the reasons why I called you."

"Okay," he grants Rebecca permission to talk. He already knows her story but listens to her attentively as she speaks. When she stops, he asks, "How do they make you feel?"

"Absolutely awful. Well, I thought those awful dreams about my husband would have stopped by now." Rebecca recounts her experiences in her dreams. Although painful, she talks to her counsellor, who supports her with this emotional experience.

"Sometimes, Rebecca, some changes in life events can evoke situations in the past, and these can manifest in our dreams. Are there any changes in your life circumstances at the moment? Is there anything bothering you?"

"Well, I'm in an extra mess because the symptoms of menopause just make me feel worse—it makes me sweat buckets, blows intolerable heat, stops me from sleeping, affects my mood, makes me feel anxious and forgetful, and brutalises me. One minute, inside, I'm calm. The next, I am extremely hot as Menopause walks, trots, then gallops and is out of control. Sometimes, Menopause does not walk. It just gallops. It is very unnerving."

"This sounds like a horse," he chuckles. "Have you spoken to your doctor about your physical symptoms?"

"Yes, I have done, and we're trying to get the symptoms sorted out so we can begin treatment."

"Good. I wish you all the best with that."

"Thank you."

"Just reflecting," Mr Xavier points to his temple. I'm thinking about the "horse Menopause" you mentioned in your dream. You said it makes you sweat buckets, and it brutalises you …"

"What are you thinking, Mr Xavier? Do you think the horse in my dreams symbolises how I feel, possibly fear and frustration of what is happening in my life now and the past failures I spoke to you about? Or is it my mind using the example of a horse to demonstrate what I am experiencing when I'm awake?" Rebecca asks.

"Um, I suppose the horse in your dream represents menopause and what you're going through."

"Yes, I believe it does. In my dream, the horse Menopause torments and brutalises me." Rebecca scratches her arm, face and neck. "My dream mirrors what is happening to me—I get extremely hot, sweat buckets, have difficulty sleeping, and my mood is affected, and my heart beats extremely fast. I feel scared and anxious and have problems with memory and concentration. Mr Xavier, menopause is real, and my symptoms are real. I am addressing those with my doctor."

"I'm pleased you've spoken to your doctor about that. You deserve the best care, Rebecca."

"Thank you." Rebecca pauses for a while. Mr Xavier gives her time to reflect on her situation and then allows her to talk. "I'm an emotional wreck at times, and this bothers me. How am I supposed to feel when horrible things come to the forefront of my mind?" Granting Rebecca permission to talk about those things that bother her, they continue their counselling session for about an hour. Rebecca is happy she called the counsellor. She always feels better once she has spoken to him. "He listens to me and doesn't judge me. I like that. I feel comfortable telling him anything that bothers me, and that helps tremendously," she says aloud.

"Once before, he told me, "Rebecca, you did your best. You cannot control what other people do. You need to forgive yourself. Sometimes, we just have to let go and accept the things we can't control in our lives, but we can control how we react."

"Exactly." Accepting the counsellor's truth,

Rebecca closes her eyes. She undertakes deep breathing exercises to gently disengage her mind from the distracting thoughts.

As she relaxes, the attack of thoughts in her head dissipates until mostly positive reviews engage her mind. In a moment of stillness, Rebecca convincingly says, "I can forgive myself, and I can accept any help offered. My children are concerned about me and want to help. I must let them, but I must also help myself."

Feeling empowered and calm, Rebecca attends her next doctor's appointment for her review. She greets the receptionist respectfully and is happy to wait until Dr Lily is ready to see her. Rebecca receives feedback from Dr Lily about her blood tests, and Dr Lily confirms that she is perimenopausal. *Ha! I'm naturally transitioning and going through my rite of passage. Although it is tough and might be more challenging, I know it is a process I must go through, although not all women will. I hope to get to the climax more robust, happier, confident, knowledgeable and resilient,* Rebecca thinks. Rebecca is satisfied that most of her blood levels are normal, although the Vitamin D count is low. She is informed by Dr Lily that she will need to be treated with a supplement.

"Why is my vitamin low, Dr Lily?"

"Rebecca, as we get older, the low oestrogen level weakens the bones. Vitamin D slows down the process that weakens the bones."

Rubbing her knee, Rebecca tells Dr Lily, "I cannot

afford for my rickety old bones to get any weaker. They are already painful enough."

"What do you do for them?"

"Exercise and Voltarol gel. I swear these help," Rebecca smiles.

Dr Lily smiles in acknowledgement. "Great. A healthy diet—oily fish like sardines, mackerel, salmon, and herring should also help. Also, continue to live an active life and exercise regularly, Rebecca, especially those activities that bear your weight, as this strengthens the bones and prevents them from breaking easily."

Rebecca speaks confidently, knowing she is already doing the right things. "I exercise regularly. And I already eat fish, liver, and red meats, but not so much for lunch and dinner. I have eggs, cereals, oats, cornmeal porridge, and yoghurt for breakfast. I also try to spend ten to thirty minutes in the sun at least twice a week as my darker skin needs a little longer under the sun's rays to absorb a decent amount of vitamin D. We girls need the extra Vitamin D because our bodies' melanin reduces our ability to absorb vitamin D."

"That's right. People with darker pigmentation are at greater risk of vitamin D deficiency."

"Yeah, I read that. That is surprising, isn't it? I thought otherwise. I have learnt so much from reading the leaflets you gave me, researching the internet, talking to other women, and listening to the Hibiscus-Rose Podcast on the BBC."

"Hibiscus-Rose Podcast?"

Rebecca informs Dr Lily about the many issues discussed regarding women, for example, menopause. "You should listen to it."

Dr Lily is grateful that Rebecca has shared the information with her. "Thank you, Rebecca. I will listen to it and share the information with my patients."

Rebecca is happy to share her knowledge. "No problem, Dr Lily. I am currently finding out more about mood swings. Remember I spoke to you about that?" Dr Lily nods. "I'm looking forward to their discussion next week about mood swings during menopause."

"Me too. Thank you. I am happy to learn more about mood swings because some studies suggest Vitamin D helps stabilize your emotions and moods."

Rebecca grins with eagerness. Besides talking to Mr Xavier about her emotions, she is willing to consider anything her doctor recommends to help. She says, "Well then, I've got to take Vitamin D. I'm ready for it. Put them here." Rebecca opens the palms of her hands towards Dr Lily.

Dr Lily smiles. "I have prescribed you Vitamin D because your level is low.

"Okay."

"I have sent the prescription to the Pharmacy. You can collect it there. Take one tablet every week for six weeks, okay? Once a week only. Please make a note of when you have taken it."

"One every week for um … six weeks," Rebecca repeats, imagining Vitamin D doing its job, she and Dr Lily are dancing happily to Soca music as they sing, "Who let the dogs out …" and Dr Lily is barking.

Mindful that Rebecca complains of brain fog, Dr Lily reminds Rebecca how to take the tablets.

"You can write the day and date when you have taken it. After completing the medicine course, make an appointment to see me. You will need to take additional Vitamin D. You can buy this over the counter when the first course is completed. Hope you feel better soon. You deserve the best, Rebecca."

Rebecca writes down the information Dr Lily gives her. She is grateful. "Thanks, Dr Lily. Will do. So glad I came to see you." Hopeful and feeling less conspicuous, she takes her sunglasses off as she leaves.

*

While she's waiting for the benefits of Dr Lily's advice, a well-balanced diet, vitamin, protein, and anti-oxidant-rich smoothies, Menopace, Frankincense, benefits of Health and Wellbeing at work, and exercise to kick in, Rebecca's children continue to explore ways to distract her from the symptoms of menopause. They conclude that their mother has been alone far too long, which might contribute to her behaviour and attitude change. Determined to find a companion for her, Shantel and RD discuss what they should do to achieve their plan.

"Mum needs a good man to distract her," RD says.

"That's exactly what I was thinking. How about Mr Adonis or Mr Oscar ..." Shantel is about to finish the list of possibilities when their mother comes into the room.

They smile at her with lips tight. Although Rebecca's children are convinced that finding a companion might help her cope with loneliness, they are embarrassed about intervening.

"I heard you mention my name. What are you saying about me now?" Rebecca asks. Her eyes narrow as she approaches them.

"All good things, Mum," RD says.

"Deffo!" Shantel agrees.

Rebecca looks at them and then up at the heavens. Whatever they are up to, she hopes it is something good. "You think I'm suffering from FOMO?" she asks, and they all laugh.

"You mean fear of missing out? It's a real thing, Mum," Shantel says softly.

"Company, Mum. Companionship," says RD. "That's what you're missing."

"It's good to spend time alone sometimes. What's wrong with that?" Rebecca asks.

"But not all the time," Shantel says.

"I've got my two lovely children who have my interest at heart and my gorgeous grandson. What or who else do I need?"

But just then, Rebecca feels a sudden need to use the toilet. Desperate to pass urine, she rushes to the bathroom and quickly tries to unbutton her trousers to pull down her undergarment. Struggling to undo the button, Rebecca squeezes her legs together, hoping to make it in time. But as she pulls down her knickers, she realises it's too late. "What the bloody hell is happening to me?" Rebecca cries despondently, sitting on the wet seat.

Chapter 11
Angel Eyes

Rebecca has begun to feel a bit better. Dr Lily's regime seems to be working, and she feels the emotional, physical and social benefits of the Calming, Mindfulness and Meditation workshops at work and the Laughter and Happiness sessions.

She's lying on the couch on a Sunday evening, reflecting after doing her exercise. "Where has the weekend gone?" Rebecca asks herself, facing the humidifier. She takes a deep breath and releases it. "We attended RD's 'Put Down the Guns, Put Down the Knives' campaign yesterday. I'm exhausted, but the march was worth it. I hope it will have an influence on young people's lives.

Besides, it was great to see PC Ginger, not so ginger now, marching with us. He's such a remarkable, considerate man. His wife died a couple of years ago, and he retired early. He's been there from the beginning, and it's lovely to see he still cares about the people in the community. Ginger has done so much

100

excellent work. I wish the other police officers would emulate Constable Ginger's behaviour rather than stop and harass every young man they meet." Rebecca yawns and stretches her arms in the air. "Yesterday was a victory. Now it's up to the young people to take the reins and make change happen."

Although they have noticed Rebecca's interest in Ginger, Shantel and RD feel he's not a good match. Since his wife died, he spends much of his time at the local pub, so they don't give up looking for a more suitable companion for their mum. They have heard through the grapevine that other lonely gentlemen in the community are looking for a companion. Still, they want to make sure and vet them first. They don't want Rebecca to repeat the turbulent relationship that she had with their father, so they talk to relatives and friends.

Finally, after having unearthed a few men they deem suitable, they try to convince her to try a date with one of them. At first, Rebecca is not having it. She hums and haws, rants and raves, but then she relents. "Okay, my darlings. Why not? I've got nothing to lose."

As Rebecca prepares for a relative's seventieth birthday party a few weeks beforehand, she plucks at the shadow above her top lip and tugs at the stray hairs under her chin. Fighting with her tweezers, she grinds her teeth in frustration. When Rebecca finally succeeds, she grins at herself in the mirror. At least she has won this battle.

Searching the wardrobe for suitable party attire, she still cannot find anything that fits. So, she goes to various dress shops but has no luck. "Too small, even smaller," she says in despair. She admires a pink-laced dress and then the bright yellow one, but she is worried that embarrassing sweat or a stain on the back might show through it, so she replaces them on the rack. She sees a green and black floral dress, but it's also too small. A black suit with an elasticated waist calls her name. "Not black again," she says, sighing. But there is nothing else, and she purchases it.

Rebecca attends the house party feeling somewhat nervous inside. She dances at home sometimes, but menopause has caused her to be cautious of exercise in public. Truth be told, Rebecca has not had the enthusiasm, energy, or desire to go out dancing for quite some time. Today, as she observes both young and older people enjoying themselves, she moves her head and legs to the music but cannot be bothered to get up and dance. Her ego tries to lift her out of the chair, but she pushes her bottom firmly into her seat in defiance.

Although battered and bruised, her ego is still intact and tries to persuade her. *Surely, I'm worth more than this, Rebecca. Dance, woman, and make me happy!* But she doesn't budge.

Rebecca observes an older gentleman called Adonis from her chair. He is trying to compete with two teenagers. It is his friend's seventieth birthday party, and he's dancing and singing to "Let's Twist Again" like he invented it.

Everyone is watching him and making comments. With his handkerchief conspicuous in his back pocket, he dances towards Rebecca.

"Hello," Rebecca says to the sharp-looking gentleman as he approaches her table.

He walks stylishly, his right foot flicking ahead of his left, singing to Kes' soca song "Hello". "Hello, hello, hello … Pretty gyal would yuh come my way."

Rebecca smiles. "You look quite official," Rebecca comments as she stands to greet him. "How are you?"

"Never better. Did you see me dancing?" He moves his head up and down, fingers clicking, his smile playful and mischievous. "I love to dance."

"Really?"

"Yes, no jokes."

"Righto," Rebecca nods.

Adonis moves his shoulder and flicks his leg. "The ladies can't stop looking at me and talking about how I move like a youngster." He spins around.

"Okay. A youngster, aye?"

He rubs his hand over his face. "And they make comments about how handsome I look. I always look good when I go out."

"Yes, sir."

"People ask about my age, and when I tell them I'm seventy, they can't believe it." He grins. "They tell me I look about forty-five."

"Forty-five?"

"Oh yes," he responds, inspecting Rebecca from head to toe. "Angel Eyes, I love a lady who also looks after herself."

"You do?"

"There is nothing more gorgeous than a beautiful lady who looks after herself," he repeats.

Rebecca scrutinises him. He waits for her to agree, but instead, she thinks, *You are so full of yourself that you're as annoying as the constant sweat dripping down my face.*

"Would you like to join me on the dance floor?" he asks. But Rebecca declines politely. She is starting to feel the heat brewing inside her, and she does not want Menopause to embarrass her in public, so she excuses herself.

Adonis advances to the dance floor with arms moving, legs kicking, and head bobbing. He looks around the room to see who is watching as he shows off his moves. The song changes, and he sings, "My boy Lollipop, you made my heart go giddy-up." He looks to where he spoke to Rebecca, moving his shoulders up and down, pushing his knees back and forth.

Rebecca's children have been observing the interaction between her and Mr Adonis from afar. As he boogies further away, they approach her to ask about their encounter.

"He's all about himself," she says. "He didn't ask me once how I was," Rebecca tells them. She is glad he left because sweat drenches the nape of her neck, and the back of her dress is soaked. She wants to go home. Astute to their mum's disapproval, her children know they must pursue another plan.

Months go by while Rebecca refuses to go out with any of the gentlemen her children suggest. They encourage her to attend social clubs, but she is not interested. She has no desire to rekindle the friendships she lost during her turbulent marital relationship. Finally, Rebecca agrees to attend a family dinner at a restaurant organised by her children. They do not tell her they have arranged for a gentleman to dine with her. Rebecca is excited because it's been a long time since the family has been out together for a meal. She wonders why Phoenix is not attending.

"He's gone out with his dad," Shantel tells her, so no suspicions are raised.

Rebecca does not ask any more questions. When the elderly man, immaculately dressed in a brown suit, cream shirt, and brown brogues, arrives at the table where Rebecca and her children are sitting, she is astounded. "Oscar! What are you doing here?" She asks, staring intently at Oscar's gold-rimmed glasses, two gold upper front teeth, a chunky, oversized gold chain, his wide double curb link bracelet and huge gold rings.

He smiles and twists his hearing aid, pats his well-groomed short moustache, and places his brown trilby on the table and sits.

Shantel and RD excuse themselves and move to a nearby table to sneak a peek at what will happen next. Rebecca clutches her purse and stands as Oscar sits opposite her, thinking she is supposed to move too.

"It's great of you to ask me to join you, Rebecca," Oscar tells her, glaring through his thick lens glasses.

She drops onto her chair with her mouth open and looks at her children in horror. She cannot believe this is happening.

"You must be at the wrong table," she tells him.

He puts his hand over his left ear because he cannot hear what she is saying. Rebecca leans forward and observes her children spying on her from a distance. They gesticulate for her to sit back down, and after some deliberation, she does.

"Children sometimes do funny things," she says, kissing her teeth.

"What?" Oscar turns up his hearing aid. It whistles so loudly that it alerts other diners as if there is an emergency.

"So, how are you, Oscar?" she asks.

"Pardon?"

"How are the children?" She raises her voice.

"Pardon?" Oscar asks, his smile open and welcoming.

They try to converse, but their conversation is strained as poor Oscar struggles to hear. But despite their initial trouble, she is tolerant, and they have an enjoyable meal. She offers to pay the bill, but Oscar declines. "It was my pleasure dining with you," he says.

Rebecca's voice is empathetic when she answers. "The pleasure was all mine."

He reads her lips and smiles.

Oscar moves Rebecca's chair back when she stands. "Thank you," she says. "You're such a gentleman."

"You're welcome," he responds. But when Oscar asks to drive Rebecca home, Shantel intervenes. "That's okay," she says. "Mum has her own car in the car park."

Chapter 12
What have I got to lose?

Rebecca is tossing and turning in her sleep. She is dreaming about Menopause again. Perplexed, she sees only the horse's head as parts of its body slowly disappear in the mist. Jumping up from her sleep, she sits up and takes deep breaths. She wonders what the significance of the dream might be. However, she does not ponder its meaning and gets out of bed and prepares for the day.

Rebecca spends the summer holidays gardening at home and in the allotment. She loves teaching but looks forward to spending time in the open air. If she could, she would convert one of those old buses, like the one she saw on George Clarkes' Amazing Spaces, or buy a campervan and travel around the UK and Europe. "My plan will have to wait," she says. "I have more important work to do."

When she returns to school, Rebecca immerses herself in ensuring the pupils achieve their full potential in all aspects of their development. She's been so busy at work that she hasn't had time to socialise. Additionally, Rebecca hasn't been on good terms with many of her female friends because of their lack of support when times were tough. But on the weekend, having embraced an attitude of forgiveness, she rekindled past friendships and moved on.

The doorbell rings. Rebecca stands still. Her heart beats fast. Panting, she takes some deep breaths and releases them slowly. She opens the door to her group of gregarious friends waiting outside, each holding a container of cooked food and salad. La Rose's eyes follow the sweat flowing from Rebecca's forehead to the tip of her nose. "Been in the rain, babes?" La Rose asks. Rebecca pats her wet face with a towel on her shoulders and laughs. She welcomes and invites her friends in. The group is gathered in Rebecca's sitting room, having a good laugh about old times while digging into some beef curry, plain rice, jollof rice, jerk chicken, lentil curry, saltfish and boiled green banana salad, and seasonal salad. Screaming in laughter, they advise Rebecca on how she can find a suitable companion.

"Ah! Rebecca, there are so many brothers around who live by themselves. Have you not met anyone yet?" Sade asks.

"Look at me," Rebecca pulls a face. "Who in their right mind would take a second look at me?"

"I'm sure there are many. Nothing's wrong with you, my dear, apart from that weave, hun," La Rose laughs. "It must go."

Rebecca lifts her weave. "Ever seen anything like that? Look what's underneath." She bites her lip and moves her fingers all along the edges of her scalp. Then she points at her belly. "And look at my tummy. It's as round and hard as a basketball. It does not belong here. If I could find that basketball player it belongs to, I would happily give it back to him, quick. If you see him, tell him I'm looking for him. And can't you see all the dark spots under my chin?"

"Where?" Sade asks. She lifts Rebecca's chin and moves it from one side to the other. Inspecting it slowly with a magnifying glass and then patting Rebecca's tummy, she says, "My Sista, there is nothing wrong with you. You're good to go."

"Tried Match Maker yet?" Eleanor says with conviction. Ava looks at her.

"What?"

"You know," her friend flashes her eyes. "Online dating." They all laugh except Ava, who is pulling a face.

"Online dating? Who in their right mind would do that?" Rebecca asks. The friends engage in a prolonged discussion about the pros and cons, and Rebecca has to admit it sounds interesting.

"Look at these two," La Rose says, pointing to her iPhone. "They met on Match Maker and are happily married."

"Mate, you should try it," Eleanor tells her. The

women keep talking and eventually convince Rebecca she should go on an internet date.

That evening, scrutinising her reflection in the mirror, Rebecca asks herself a question. "Shall I go on this online date? What have I got to lose? If I don't try, I will never know." She winks slyly, but her confidence dips when she checks the side view. Should she actually pursue this? She paces around the room, her head full of doubt.

Do I want another man in my life? Do I really want to have a relationship with someone else after the disaster of my marriage to Blake? Should I disturb the status quo? Who will I meet, and what will be the outcome? Will Menopause attack me on the date?

As she sits facing the computer with trepidation, Rebecca contemplates the implications of accessing the site. Sweating, she leaves it for another day, but days become weeks. Finally, after months of deliberation, she accesses the dating site only to close it down immediately. But she's curious about what she might see, so Rebecca finds the courage again. With trembling hands, she completes her profile and the other requirements. Lost in thought, she is shaken as her daughter walks into the room and calls her by name. "Rebecca?"

Shantel looks at her with suspicion. "What are you doing, Mum? Got a boyfriend online?" she asks teasingly.

Rebecca doesn't know how to respond. Thinking on her feet, she quickly redirects her browser to a gardening website.

"Boyfriend! You must be joking. I ain't got time for that. Looking for some new plants for the garden, that's all," she says. "It's about time I pay more attention to the garden and the allotment. Too many weeds, don't you think? Doesn't this peony look beautiful? And what about this lovely rose?"

"Too many weeds, for sure. We need some beautiful flowers," Shantel nods, not any wiser to her mother's truth. She sits with Rebecca while talking about their day and glances at the screen as she leaves. She winks at her mum.

Despite her apprehension, Rebecca visits the site the following week. Five gentlemen have expressed an interest, and Rebecca is nervously excited. Moving the bar from left to right and right to left and left to right again. Rebecca scrutinises the men eager to befriend her. She examines their profile pictures, ages, backgrounds, hobbies, occupations, and salaries.

She spends the next few weeks communicating with the candidates online. She does not tell her children, but excitedly, she confides in her friends, who are delighted for her. Some have had successful online relationships and are enjoying happy, healthy marriages. All except Ava, whose knight in shining armour was not the person she expected.

Rebecca continues communicating with three gentlemen. She swipes left to two of them. Over time, she swipes right to one man who catches her eye, and Rebecca's keen to learn more about him. The gentleman that she has chosen is very complementary. As a result, Rebecca is happier and more confident in herself. He has the gift of the gab, and they regularly converse on FaceTime.

"You're really that age, beautiful?" he asks her.

"Yep," she says.

"From your profile picture, you can't be a day over thirty-five."

Rebecca's eyes twinkle in happiness. "Thirty-five? You've got to be kidding. Stop it, Beau."

"Seriously, no jokes. I mean every word I say. This gentleman never lies," he boasts.

Beau's bass-baritone voice hypnotises her, and Rebecca wants to hear more. She spends hours talking to him, and at the end of their latest conversation, she arranges to meet the gentleman in person. Yet, although she trusts his voice, she is still mindful of the potential risks involved and decides it will have to be in a public place if she makes contact. So, they decide on a local pub, and Beau will wear red for identification.

Rebecca has a sleepless night for fear of meeting someone new and of the bothersome Menopause attacking her in the interim. She hopes that the brute will give her a break today. Rebecca leaves home with trepidation. She brings her best friend, La Rose, as a backup plan, but they part at the door. As planned, an older, handsome man enters the pub wearing a red shirt and red cap. Rebecca's eyes are directed towards his red trousers. The bottom of his red trousers lies above the top of his long red socks. He is walking towards her. Rebecca covers her face in shock and advances towards La Rose, who is smirking. Fortunately, he walks past Rebecca towards a young woman who greets him excitedly. Rebecca is happy for him. Her cheeks rise as she observes a handsome brunette in his forties, true to his profile, wearing a red cap and top. He is holding a huge bunch of red roses.

Rebecca likes the look of him but is still slightly uncertain. When he walks toward her, her heart races. But when he asks her if she is Rebecca, she says, "Rebecca, who?"

His baritone-base voice plays music in her ears. "Rebecca Dawson, of course."

"Rebecca Dawson? Sorry, I don't know anyone of that name." She marches to the corner and sits down at La Rose's table.

Her friend giggles, but Rebecca does not think the situation is funny. "I had high hopes for this man, but you have to be so careful," she tells La Rose over coffee. "He looked great, though. But you never know who you are going to meet. They might look good, but you don't know their intentions."

But deep inside, Rebecca wonders why she was so afraid of getting to know such an obviously compliant gentleman.

Back home, Rebecca deletes the Match Maker website. She sleeps restlessly, her mind occupied with the potentially dangerous position she could have put herself in earlier. Her heart pounds, and her head throbs, imagining what could have happened. She didn't know the man, but she agreed to meet him.

Silly me. No one should compromise their safety like that. Online dates are not for everyone. Sometimes, it works out, and sometimes, it doesn't.

Rebecca is thankful she brought her trusted friend, La Rose with her. Her mind relaxes as she thinks of alternative ways of keeping engaged besides dating. She re-evaluates what she needs to do to look after herself properly.

Chapter 13

Alternative Therapy

Rebecca has decided that focusing on nutrition, exercise, and a healthy lifestyle will keep her fit and happy. She dances around the house, singing her favourite song, "Feelin' Hot, Hot, Hot."

"Shantel, I have something to tell you," Rebecca tells her daughter, reaching for her hand.

The music is loud, so Shantel cannot hear her mum's words. "What are you saying, Mum?" Shantel asks. She, too, is moving to the music.

Rebecca turns the music off. "Shantel, sit down," her mum says. Shantel squints. Her mind is racing with speculations as she wonders what her mum is about to tell her. She forms a narrative in her head.

Lately, Mum has been happily singing and dancing around the house, with the music much louder than she is used to. She has even been dancing to the "Migraine Skank" and "Party Hard" like a youngster. I wonder what is going on. I'm happy for her, of course. Maybe she wants to buy a new car, buy a bungalow, go on a cruise, move to France, or she's found a younger companion. After all, she is in her midlife phase of life, which is often challenging. So, I'm not sure what she is going to tell me. We have been trying to find her a companion but have not succeeded. She keeps praising and talking incessantly about her forty-something, fit, young gym instructor. Maybe she wants to tell me about him. So Shantel sits in readiness with ears erect to hear what her mum has to say.

"A few weeks ago, I met up with …"

Prepare for it, Shantel.

Shantel does not allow her to continue. Her mind is focused on this probable younger companion.

"With whom?" Shantel holds her breath.

"La Rose." Relieved, Shantel releases her breath and lets her mum speak.

"We had such an interesting discussion. It was amazing."

Wait for it.

"About Phyto…" She does not let her mum finish speaking.

Sounds Greek to me. "Who?"

"Phyto N..."

"Phyto Nikos?" Shantel interjects.

Her mum pushes her head back, her forehead is pulled back with her mouth hung open.

"Who is that? Your gym instructor?"

Her mother laughs.

"What, Shantel?" Her mother asks.

Shantel is still making assumptions in her head again. I bet she is about to tell me, "*He is younger than me*".

La Rose has been educating me about phytonutrients."

"Phyto who?"

"Phytonutrients. Babes, these chemicals in foods …"

"Chemicals!" Shantel interjects.

"Good chemicals, you know, natural ones produced by plants that are good for you, babes. They protect the plants from diseases, insects and the sun. They are healthy for our body and mind and also protect us from many diseases. Isn't that great, Shantel? You find them in red, orange, green and yellow fruits and vegetables, berries, leafy vegetables, sweet potatoes, oranges and edible flowers, and it's never too early to start eating them, my dear."

Without warning, Rebecca suddenly feels hot. Preparing for a brutal attack from Menopause, she fans herself with some leaflets. But it's only a passing phase, and after it's over, she puts a shawl over her shoulders and continues talking. "You should start eating plenty of these now, so when your turn comes, your menopause symptoms will be less vicious than mine."

Shantel pulls her lips back. "Me? Eek! Perish the thought. Don't want to think about that right now. Much too young."

"My girl, you're never too young to think about menopause, seriously. The more you know about it, the more prepared you are, the better you'll be able to deal with menopause, my dear," Rebecca says.

"Okay, if you say so, Mum. You constantly say knowledge is power, and I have to agree."

Rebecca is excited. She has a wealth of knowledge that she is determined to share with her daughter. She wants her to be equipped for that phase of her life when the time comes.

"My only daughter, you must continue to eat a healthy diet, including many fruits, vegetables, whole grains and food rich in calcium and vitamin D, milk and milk products, and green leafy vegetables. Here's a list. If you eat them, you might not be so badly affected by the symptoms of menopause when you reach my age."

"Really?"

"Yes, prevention is better than cure, Shantel. You cannot prevent menopause, but you might be able to deal with the brutality of menopause. Amazingly, Shantel, you can also eat foods that contain phytoestrogens to help you do that."

"What's that, Mum? First phytonutrients, now phytoestrogens. I'm confused."

"Babes, don't look at me like that. What I'm saying to you is that some plants produce food that contains oestrogen, which keeps our natural hormones balanced. Can you imagine that? When we eat food containing phytoestrogens, our bodies respond as if oestrogen is present."

"Mum, what are you on about?"

"Let me make it clearer, my dear. In other words,

Shantel, eating foods with phytoestrogens, like foods with soy, soya milk, soya flour, tofu, pulses, beans and oils, apparently reduce the frequency of hot flushes in women."

Shantel's mum shoves some grains into her hand. Determined that her daughter does not suffer the same fate as her, she tries to convince her to eat nutritious seeds.

"Try flax, sunflower, and pumpkin seeds, which are also good for you. They have phytoestrogen in them, too. And even white foods as well, you know. Foods like onions, garlic, and olive oil are also very good for you."

Rebecca hands Shantel a bag filled with onions and garlic. "Start eating more of these now, and you'll feel the benefit, for sure," Rebecca tells her daughter.

Overwhelmed by the information her knowledgeable, enthusiastic and loving mum has given her, Shantel tells her, "Thank you for the info, Mum. That's excellent advice, but that's a lot of information for me to take in right now. I will read the leaflets you gave me and search the internet for more information." Rebecca nods and leaves the kitchen just as RD rings the doorbell. When Shantel opens the door, her brother asks, "What are these?" He inspects her palm.

"Seeds."

"Obviously, but why? Are you feeding the birds?" He asks, looking around for the feathered friends.

"Our mum said I've got to eat plenty of them. Ahem, where are your keys? You know how she hates opening the door for you."

RD's nose twitches. "Where is she, and what's that smell?" he asks.

"It's Frankincense, and she's upstairs."

"Frankincense?"

"Another of Mum's remedies for dealing with her menopausal symptoms. She swears that it works and claims that she has no more problems with memory loss since she has been using it. And trust me, RD, she is as sharp as a tack these days! Even you cannot challenge her at chess. She is too good."

"We'll see," RD says, determined. "I like that Frankincense. It smells nice. What other ailments does it cure?" he asks, laughing. "I have a slight headache from work, you know."

Shantel looks around, ensuring that Rebecca does not hear his sarcastic tone. "No jokes," she says. "If Mum hears you dissing her Frankincense, she'll go ballistic."

RD is distracted as he spies a glass of green liquid on the table behind Shantel. "What's that green stuff?" he asks.

"That's another thing Mum swears helps relieve her menopause symptoms. It's a blend of green fruits and vegetables. She says it's full of vitamins, proteins and healthy fats."

"I didn't know fats are healthy?"

Pulling a face at her brother, she says, "Yeh, man. Fats in nuts, seeds, avocados, coconut milk and cold press coconut oil are healthy."

RD cautiously takes a sip. "Yum. Mummy has good taste."

Shantel laughs, "You mean Mum?"

"Yes, Mum. Recipe, please," he slurps the drink.

"Well," says Shantel, "Mum makes a blended concoction of green pawpaw, fresh lemon juice, spinach, sometimes kale or bok choi, avocado, one teaspoon of coconut oil, and flaxseeds. She adds one glass of coconut water and one tablespoon of maca powder."

"Recipe noted. I must maca smoothie like that," RD smirks.

"Make, aye," Shantel says, and they both laugh. "Bro, no jokes. Maca is a superfood that apparently has medicinal and health benefits. Apparently, it improves fertility, sexual function, energy, memory and learning."

"Providing Mum takes it for energy, memory and learning, I'm all for that."

"Power to Rebecca. Power to Mum," Shantel says.

Shantel and RD stare at Rebecca as she comes downstairs. She's wearing floral-patterned leggings, a crop top, and trainers with a yellow towel around her neck. Shantel sings the chorus to Alicia Keys' song, "Girl On Fire," and RD raps, "This girl is on fire." Rebecca laughs and sings with Shantel with her hands up in the air. She lifts her leg up and moves her hips. RD and Shantel giggle with happiness and contentment.

RD kisses his mum and compliments her on how amazing and chilled she looks. "I must get some Frankincense and make that green smoothie drink. I want to look as good as you. Anything else you recommend?"

Rebecca smiles as she dances her way to the door. "No time to talk today," she says. "I'm off to the gym. Ta ta"

"Gym?" RD asks.

"You should come with me one day. You'd love it." She waves goodbye but suddenly turns around swiftly, standing in the doorway with one hand on the back of her head and the other on her hips. RD and Shantel wonder what is happening. RD wonders whether she is going to dance to the migraine skank like Shantel's childhood friend, Bianca. He has not seen her for several years, but he can imagine her whining to the ground with one hand on her head and the other on her hips.

On the other hand, Shantel fears that Menopause is up to his tricks again. She hopes that after so much progress, her mum is not lashed by Menopause again. That would be a disaster. Shantel is about to rush towards her but stands holding a chair with her mouth open as Rebecca raps, her hands moving in every direction.

"Fit, fabulous and fifty,
> This is me.
> I stand with my feet firmly planted
> Like an old oak tree.
> I can move like any teenager.
> And delegate like any competent manager.
> I am flexible and firm,
> And I can hold my own.
> Firm, fit and fifty,
> That's me."

Rebecca looks at her children with a broad grin. Self-satisfied, she does not say anything. She jumps over the doorway and closes the door behind her.

RD looks at Shantel, perplexed. "What in the world was that about? What happened to my mother?"

"Our mother, Rebecca? I told you she is feeling herself again. She has found her old self again. Positivity all the way, I hear Mum repeating right now. Seeing old Mum active and agile again was great, but I hope she doesn't do that publicly."

"Me, too. That wouldn't do much for my image, would it?" RD snorts.

RD and Shantel look at their mother's photo and laugh at each other.

"Mum is into much more stuff to help herself—relaxation, healthy eating, yoga, daily brisk walks, gym, chess, colour therapy..."

"A busy lady, our Mum. I wish she could focus on just one thing. Did you say colour therapy? What the heck is that?"

"You live in colour, see, breathe, think, dream, and eat and drink colour. In fact, surround yourself with colour, which will positively affect your mental and physical well-being. Mum said you must wear colours, drink and eat colourful fruits and vegetables, and meditate with colour. They even use coloured lights in this form of therapy. It's all about colour my brother, and Mum swears it works.

RD scratches his head. "It's all a mystery to me, Sis."

"Me, too. I need to read more about colour therapy. I've sent you the Google link. Read the info later, Bro."

RD reads out loud. "Colour for Health | Get. gg - Getselfhelp.co.uk. Ok, thanks, Sis. I'm already breathing in colour." He sniffs the remaining green drink in his glass, takes a deep breath, holds it and breathes out. "I like it."

"Bro, can you believe it?"

What is she about to tell me? Mum has a young boyfriend? RD waits in anticipation.

"Mum is even having swimming lessons, too."

RD breathes out deeply, relieved. "Didn't think

Mum had an interest in swimming!"

Shantel does not bother to tell RD that Rebecca's menstrual periods have stopped. She knows he wouldn't want to speak about that. "Yeah. Mum is determined to be a proficient swimmer. She likes to excel in everything she does and is always keen to learn more. She has even been to menopause retreats. She wants to share her story about her experience of menopause because she does not want any women to suffer in silence with the symptoms of menopause. She wants to educate women and their families to empower them so they can take control of their lives. I don't know where she gets the time and energy. Still, Rebecca says her new purpose is to reclaim the special person buried inside her, and she's buzzing like a busy bee."

"Buzzzz. Really?"

"Yeah. There's no stopping Mum. She considered going on HRT, Hormone Replacement Therapy. She had spoken to her doctor about that but heard some bad reports and declined to take it. She told me a story about a woman who left East London. Apparently, she lost her way on the train. After about two hours, she ended up on Nomansland Common in Hertfordshire instead of Whitechapel because of messed up hormones."

RD looks at his sister in disbelief. "It's a mystery to me."

"So she said RD. So Mum isn't going to take

a chance. Now, she's trying alternative natural treatments instead of HRT and swears by the results. She says HRT works for some and not for others, but she would not dissuade any women from having it. They should be able to choose."

RD nods. "Good for her. I'm glad Mum is feeling better. Whatever works for her, I'm all for that."

"Rebecca deserves the best. She does so much for others, including us." Shantel winks. "It's time for it to be about her now. We must find her a man, a gentleman."

Chapter 14
Embracing Menopause

In her most recent dream, Rebecca puts her arms around Menopause's arched neck and hugs the troublesome stallion. He snorts and nuzzles her armpit. They seem to have reached a truce, and Rebecca feels empowered and happy now that her nemesis has settled down. Wanting to share her knowledge and experience with other women struggling with menopause and address the associated taboos, Rebecca asks Shantel for advice.

"I want to raise awareness about menopause, educate and inspire women, and empower them to retake control of their lives. I want them to embrace it as I did. Mind you, it wasn't easy," she says passionately. "They need to know that it is a natural process that many women will go through. The majority will have a traumatic time, and a few won't. Things can be so different if we know about it, accept it, and then deal with it. Knowledge is Power."

Shantel agrees. "Yes, Mum, you're right. I

think education about menopause should start early by explaining the symptoms and behaviour change so the children can understand what their sisters, mothers, grandmothers, aunts and other relatives are going through. But first, they must be taught about the benefits of healthy eating, exercising and healthy lifestyle choices. Why don't we start a chat group online? Women as young as me also need to know about menopause to prepare for it. We need to confidently talk about menopause rather than referring to it as "that thing". We might be able to engage parents, carers and educators so they can educate their children."

After further discussion and research, they start the 'Hibiscus-Rose Menopause and Me' chat room. As Rebecca tries to help the women in the group get a grip, she shares her story, and the women listen and respond with their own.

Holly:> The sweat comes from nowhere. I am drenched one minute, and the next, the sweat disappears.

Julia:> I thought I was the only one. How come that happens?

Rebecca:< It's all because of menopause which marks the end of us having periods or the time leading to that point. Although menopause can be brutal, it is a natural part of ageing.

Julia:> Tell you the truth, I am okay with that. I wouldn't miss it. It is so unpredictable. One day, there's a drip, drip, then gush, gush, then the period goes on vacation for two months. Then it's back with a vengeance, causing havoc. This is so annoying and distressing.

Rebecca:<Yes, it can be, Julia. The imbalance of hormones during menopause causes havoc in our bodies, leaving us women feeling weak and sometimes useless. The constant sweat, intense heat, chills, mood swings, and anxiety can be distressing.

La Rose:> Hormones?

Rebecca:< Yes, my dear. It's all about the hormones.

Holly:> Oh, I see. That's why I'm boiling hot one minute, and the next, I'm freezing cold. Now, I can explain to my husband, children, family, friends, and colleagues why I need to be by myself sometimes.

Ava:> I can't sleep, either.

La Rose:> Me too. Worse of all is that I have no interest in you know what.

Holly:> Sex! I'm not shy to talk about it. I'm not enjoying it, and I have no desire for it.

Rebecca:< You mean you have a low sex drive, loss of libido? Low levels of hormones cause that, too. It's all about hormones, mate. You are not alone. Women affected by the symptoms of menopause should not be embarrassed to talk about them.

Holly:> So, those hormones do a great job at normal levels, but when they are low, they cause chaos in my body, so it's not my fault I am emotional? Holly sniffles.

Rebecca:< Yes, Holly. We hear you. Bless you.

We hear all of you. Yes, shout about menopause! No, Holly, It is not your fault. Menopause is a fact of life. Mind you, I'm not saying it is easy. Most of us women will be affected by menopause. It ain't easy for many women. However, we must accept that menopause exists, and therefore, we can deal with it through acceptance. Menopause exists. You see, Holly, decreased levels of hormones affect our bodies, emotions, and sex drive. And when the vagina becomes dry, it makes it unpleasant to have sex.

La Rose:> Ouch!

Rebecca:< I hear you, La Rose. Over-the-counter water-based lubricants and some vaginal hormonal creams can help. For some of you, the hormone testosterone might boost or restore your low sex drive. You can ask your doctor to prescribe it, if you wish. Happy Days! There are other ways of enjoying sex: massage, caressing, sensual baths ...

La Rose:> Yay! Rebecca, stress, tiredness and sleeplessness don't help, either. I need more help.

Rebecca:< You are right, La Rose. You can discuss your symptoms with your doctor or another health professional. Still, some of you might be able to manage your symptoms by yourself with some changes like eating a well-balanced diet, exercising, meditating, and some simple lifestyle changes. Drinking more water is one of the simplest changes that can help relieve some symptoms during menopause. For some of you, your doctor might suggest HRT to help with those awful symptoms of menopause. Listen attentively to the information they give you, and make your informed decision, but let me forward you some PDF information that offers helpful alternative herbal remedies. They work for some but, unfortunately, not for all. But you'll never know unless you try them. Prevention, my dear, is better than cure.

Ladies, love and appreciate yourself. Pamper yourself. Be kind to yourself. Find time to read a book. Have you read The Alchemist by Paulo Coelho? It is an inspiring book. There is so much you can learn from reading this book. Life is a journey. We must learn to navigate it. There is so much to learn about ourselves. I must say that although many of us will go through this turbulent journey of menopause, some women will struggle through this natural transition and right of passage but arrive at the climax as strong, resilient, confident, assertive and knowledgeable individuals.

Remove that veil. Don't stay silent. Talk about how you feel. Shout about menopause, my friends.

The group continues their sessions, and Rebecca allows them to discuss their difficulties. As the group listens attentively, Rebecca advises them to be courageous and talk to family and friends who will listen about what they are going through. She tells them they can also speak to a health professional, including a menopause specialist nurse, or a complementary or an alternative therapist about the symptoms and difficulties when they feel the time feels right.

"Rebecca, you're a God send. Since our discussions, I spoke to my doctor, who referred me for 'Talk Therapy'. I talk with them about my troubles with menopause. They listen, and slowly, I am getting there." Holly says.

"Good on you. Wishing you all the best. You deserve the best, my dear," Rebecca tells her. The chat room is full of applause for Holly.

"I thank everyone for attending and sharing your views and experience. Thank you for your support. I will also forward some helpful information about menopause and some menopause support groups."

The discussion continues for about twelve months before Rebecca feels it is time for Shantel, with help from Holly, La Rose, and Julia, to take control of the group. The chat now includes the voices of concerned younger women like Daisy, and Shantel feels that she has started something worthwhile to benefit her friends, old and new.

Rebecca is in a deep sleep. She dreams about Menopause with its jaw hanging loose. She covers her face to protect her from its wrath, but it does not brutalise or torment her. It is calm and controlled. Its soft, round eyes gleam at her. Rebecca smiles as she slumbers into a deeper, more comfortable night's sleep.

The following morning, Rebecca wakes up, realising she has not had any hot flushes for quite some time. Brushing her teeth, she stops momentarily and questions her reflection in the mirror.

"Where has Menopause gone?" she asks. Then she snorts. "Well, wherever it is, I hope that rascal stays there indefinitely."

*

Considerable time has passed, and Rebecca stands like a stork in front of her mirror. Her full lips are upturned, the corner of her lips crinkle, and her green eyes gleam in the daylight. Standing balanced, she slowly teases her leg into the leg of her trousers. She puts one leg down and gently lifts the other leg. Still balanced, she glides her other leg in. Standing and moving in different stances, she curls her fingers playfully and buttons her trousers. Flirting with her top, Rebecca places her arm into the sleeve of her top, not afraid a conflict will ensue. She laughs aloud as she remembers her previous experience of the arm-sleeve war. Thrilled with the result, Rebecca wears her new pink and gold shoes and dances out of the house.

The Dawson family sits proudly at Phoenix's graduation. Elegantly dressed in her pink trousers, floral top, and gold and pink shoes, Rebecca smiles in anticipation. Seated beside RD and Shantel, she runs her fingers through her short, curly, natural hair peppered with grey streaks. She laughs as she remembers the long, curly weave that once covered her thinning hair.

Her pink lips curve up as a tall gentleman sits beside her. As he smiles, he exposes a gap in his teeth. "Is your son or daughter graduating today?" he asks, scanning her.

"Pardon me?"

"Your son or daughter, graduating?"

"My grandson, bless him," Rebecca responds.

She looks at the silver-headed gentleman with his bowler hat sitting proudly on his lap. His grey suit and grey bow tie complement his hair.

"Grandmother! You don't look old enough." Rebecca smiles.

The gentleman smiles and nods. "My granddaughter is graduating in Engineering, and I am so proud of her.

"Good for her, and good for you. Congratulations."

"And yours?"

"My grandson, Phoenix, has a First Class Degree in Accounts and Finance. He wants to be the Chancellor of the Exchequer."

"Good for him. If he believes it, he can achieve it."

My sentiments precisely. Positivity all the way, Rebecca thinks.

Rebecca takes out her powder puff, brushes some powder on her cheeks, and looks at the gentleman with eyes gleaming. The ceremony begins, and they end their conversation abruptly.

RD and Shantel whisper about the older gentleman sitting beside their mother. "They look like an ideal couple," Shantel says.

"Do you think we can get them together?"

"We can only try. You said you know him, and he is a good man. God knows Mum deserves one."

"Well, we won't know until we do. Until such time, let's celebrate Phoenix's achievement."

"Yes, let's."

Rebecca waits nervously to hear her grandson's name. She smiles while Shantel and RD clap loudly and shout, "Well done, Phoenix. **WHOOP! WHOOP!**"

Once the ceremony ends, the family pounces on Phoenix, hugging, kissing, and praising him. He shrinks in embarrassment at the many people watching them.

"We knew you would do it," Rebecca tells him. "Bravo, my favourite grandson! You believed you could do it, and you achieved your goal."

"We are so proud of you," Shantel tells him, beaming with pride.

"So proud of you," Silk tells his son, beaming happily.

"Thanks for believing in me, everybody. Thank you, Mum, Dad, Uncle and Grandma," Phoenix says.

RD taps him on the back and ruffles his hair. "Well

done, Son. I knew you would do it. Forward you go!"

Rebecca walks around the shopping centre with her trolley a few days later. As she turns a corner, she collides with another one driven by the man she spoke briefly to at her grandson's graduation.

"Hello again," she says.

"Oh, hi," he says. "I guess I was daydreaming. I'm still in awe of my granddaughter's achievement. She is the first to graduate in the family. Bless her."

"Again, congratulations."

"Thank you, ma'am. Sorry …"

Rebecca waits for him to speak.

"Didn't introduce myself." Stretching his hand, he says, "Sebastian Boniface Jones, ma'am."

"Nice to meet you, Mr Jones," Rebecca says. "Maybe we'll meet again sometime." His eyes follow her trail visually until she disappears down another aisle. *Fine lady*, he thinks to himself.

Rebecca doesn't notice Sebastian Boniface Jones. As she enters the community centre where RD is holding a meeting, the gentleman walks up to the podium and sits beside her son. He takes the microphone and talks eloquently about his empathy for young people and how he will continue to support the community financially.

With passion in his voice, RD expresses the need for the community to work together to benefit their young people. He urges the elders to continue having meaningful dialogues with the youth to empower them to make changes in their lives that will make a difference.

"We need to stop gun and knife crimes. Together, we can make a difference," RD expresses.

The people present are broken into groups, and Rebecca and Mr Jones are allocated to the same group. Listening respectfully as they make their points, they are encouraged by each other's words.

They meet again when Rebecca attends other events launched by her son, and over time, they become friends.

Chapter 15

Happy At Last

Rebecca and her "friend" SBJ have been spending a lot of quality time together working on the allotment, visiting museums, attending the library, swimming, experimenting with creating new meals, visiting their families, and simply staying home and watching movies.

The children are happy for Rebecca. "Mum has never looked better," Shantel says.

RD nods. "Yes, I agree. Rebecca is even more beautiful than she was before. She looks so relaxed. The two are so well suited for each other."

"Bright and light clothing all the time," Shantel says, smiling. "Mum is our superhero!"

*

RD stands outside the front door, his nostrils dancing to the smell of his mother's cooking. He doesn't ring the bell but puts his key in the lock as instructed. As the door swings open, he rushes eagerly towards the kitchen, drawn by the tantalising aroma.

RD kisses Rebecca. "Smells delicious. What are you cooking today, Mum?" he asks. "What can I do to help?"

Rebecca directs her eyes to the kitchen sink full of used pots and utensils. Intuitive to her wishes, RD washes them while watching the hob and his mother. He does not want the food to burn today. He wants his taste buds to sing happily to another one of his mother's delicious Creole meals.

Rebecca suspects RD's insinuation and leaves the kitchen briefly. As she turns her back, RD uncovers the pots. He grins, exposing his perfectly shaped teeth to the contents. Satisfied all is going well, RD leaves to meet his mum in the sitting room.

"WOW! Rebecca," he says as he observes his mother. She's wearing a yellow linen top and white trousers. Her lips are ruby red, and her eyelids are tinted green. "You look great, Mum. The paint on your eyelids complements your eyes."

"Paint! No, it's eyeshadow, dear."

"So, where are you off to?" he asks.

Rebecca's lips part in a smile. "None of ya business," she tells him.

Momentarily, the doorbell rings, and Rebecca rushes to answer it. Mr SBJ enters, and she kisses him on the cheek. The corners of his lips lift when he says, "Hello, Rebecca," his voice is deep and enchanting.

"Good afternoon, RD."

"Good afternoon, SBJ," RD laughs and fist-pumps him. He's happy to see his mum's new "friend" and is even more delighted to see the contentment on his mother's face.

"Make yourself at home, sir," Rebecca says.

As SBJ enters the sitting room, he removes his jacket and places it at the back of the chair. He flicks the braces attached to his high-waisted trousers. Advancing into the kitchen, he turns up the cuff of the sleeve of his pristine shirt and washes his hands. After wiping the granite worktop with warm, soapy water, he takes a cabbage, carrots, and spring onions from the fridge. Washing them, he begins his culinary adventure.

Whilst moving his legs to the rhythm of "Better Days Are Coming" by Jimmy Cliff, SBJ grates the carrots and cuts up the cabbage and spring onion. Adding salad cream and mayonnaise, he tastes the content and smiles with satisfaction. "Mmmm."

"SBJ!" Phoenix says with excitement as he enters the kitchen. "Hope you made that special coleslaw again. Are we playing the number game later?"

"Sure, Phoenix, I'm looking forward to it. It's always a pleasure to win a round from a graduate in Accounts and Finance and future Chancellor of the Exchequer," he teases.

Phoenix grins. "Good luck. You can only try."

Pleasure lights up Shantel's face as she regards her mother's demeanour. "Good to see you as always, SBJ," she says.

They all sit at the expansive dining table to enjoy a family meal of rice and peas, garlic and spring onion stuffed chicken, stew chicken, macaroni cheese, curry goat, roast potatoes, SBJ's unique coleslaw, and cinnamon and apple crumble and custard. RD's taste buds leap in excitement. "For what we are about to receive, may the Lord make us truly thankful. Amen!" He says speedily.

"Amen!" the others respond, and they tuck into their meal.

"Stop chapping your mouth like that, RD," his sister tells him, and they all laugh.

"Thank you, Mum and SBJ," RD grins as he devours the home-cooked meal. He laughs as he continues. "… For the delicious meal handed down by my grandmother's recipe cooked by my mother's "own hands" with help from a friend. Bless the hands that made the food."

"Thank you, Grandma and SBJ," Phoenix says. "This food is delicious. I always told you Grandma was the best cook ever."

Rebecca smiles in acknowledgement, and Shantel nods, her mouth too full to talk.

RD picks up his Tupperware container and grins with happiness.

The next time RD puts on a march to address the pressing issue of gun and knife crimes in the community, his mother and Sebastian Boniface Jones stand beside him. They are holding hands, and Phoenix's fingers are entwined in his mother's and father's as they shout in unison with the youth group.

> "Put down the gun,
> Put down the knives,
> We have to preserve our lives."

THE END

Epilogue

Rebecca stands beside her blue campervan wearing a yellow hat, a red rain mac, and green Wellington boots. It is pouring rain. Full of energy, she dances in the rain around the campervan like she is being filmed for the movie "*Singin' in the Rain*". With vigour, she sings, "I'm singing in the rain. I'm happy again." Her children laugh.

Rebecca removes her mac and flings it on the back seat. She waves goodbye to her family as she leaves with SBJ for their long-awaited adventure around the United Kingdom. Pressing her foot on the accelerator, she breathes in the fresh air of the countryside. Rebecca exhales slowly, admiring the beautiful flowers in bloom, tall trees, stunning landscapes, scenic cliffs, undulating hills, and valleys. Tranquil and content with the solid companionship of SBJ, Rebecca feels free at the same time.

"Angel Eyes," SBJ says, placing his hand on her thigh, "there is no place I would rather be." Looking deeply into her sparkling eyes, he kisses Rebecca's cheek, and she smiles.

"And there is no place I would rather be than with

you, Mr Sebastian Boniface Jones," she says. Rebecca sings the lyrics to, 'I Can See Clearly Now' by Jimmy Cliff. SBJ listens with joy in his heart. Together, they sing along with Pharrell's song "Happy" on the radio, perfectly describing Rebecca's liberated mind.

SOME

Symptoms of Menopause

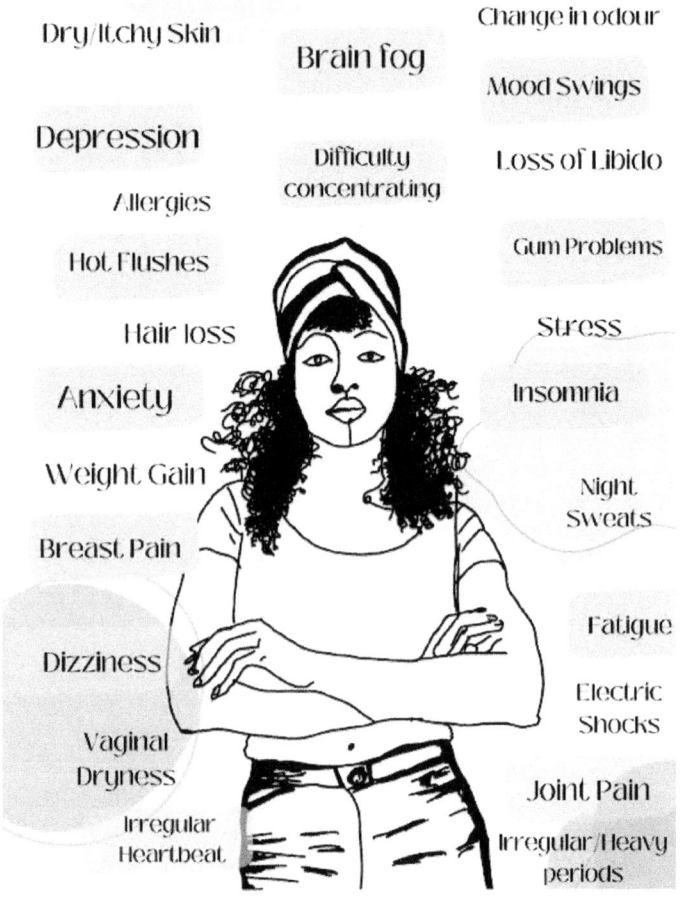

Dry/Itchy Skin
Brain fog
Change in odour
Mood Swings
Depression
Difficulty concentrating
Loss of Libido
Allergies
Hot Flushes
Gum Problems
Hair loss
Stress
Anxiety
Insomnia
Weight Gain
Night Sweats
Breast Pain
Fatigue
Dizziness
Electric Shocks
Vaginal Dryness
Joint Pain
Irregular Heartbeat
Irregular/Heavy periods

Illustrated by Alicia Melanie

Let's Talk About Menopause

The Change

"That's the only way that Menopause has been described for most of my life, with the only symptom mentioned being 'hot flushes'. It's only now, at 42, that I am starting to hear the lived stories of those who have been through it, gone through it or are preparing for it, as without them, I would be so unprepared for what is to come. We need to hear Rebecca's story and the stories of countless others to understand our bodies and minds and prepare for something natural that will look and feel different for each of us who will go through it and be empowered to speak about it LOUDLY."

Tana-Rose Brill

Menopause

"I understand menopause is a normal part of growing older. It is nothing to be embarrassed or ashamed about because it's just a part of being a woman, and your body is adjusting to its new phase of life. Menopause happens in life and can be a trying time for some. Just know that you aren't the only one going through it. I believe one should take it in their stride and access and explore any pharmaceutical or holistic options available. Talk to your doctor and other people about menopause and what you are going through, and be an open book; in doing so, you may help yourself and someone else."

Anelise Phillip-Mathurin

"It is a sad truth that menopause is so taboo. This is a universal experience for every woman in their life. We should know and learn more about this. I have heard and seen the different ways many women experience menopause. It appears to be an out-of-body experience. Women should have examples of how to cope, talk through and come to terms with menopause."

Alicia Melanie

Menopause support groups:

Menopause - Symptoms - NHS (https://www.nhs.uk/conditions/menopause/symptoms/)

Menopause - Help and support - NHS (https://www.nhs.uk/conditions/menopause/help-and-support/)

Early menopause (premature menopause) - Support Network (www.earlymenopause.com/)

Menopause - Support networks for menopausal women (https://healthtalk.org/menopause/support-networks-for-menopausal-women)

The Menopause Charity - Menopause Facts, Advice and Support (www.themenopausecharity.org)

Menopause in Ethnic Minority Women (https://thebms.org.uk/wp-content/uploads/2023/06/20-BMS-TfC-Menopause-in-ethnic-minority-women-JUNE2023-A.pdf)

Menopause - Overview (https://healthtalk.org/introduction/menopause/)

Holland and Barrett Menopause Support (www.https://www.hollandandbarrett.com/info/menopause-support/)

NHS England - Supporting our NHS people through menopause: guidance for line managers and colleagues (https://www.england.nhs.uk/long-read/supporting-our-nhs-people-through-menopause-guidance-for-line-managers-and-colleagues/)

The Author

Yvonne Laurencia Phillip RGN RM RHV BSC (Hons) PGCE was born in Guadeloupe, West Indies. She is a daughter of Dominican parents and is one of six children. She went to primary school in Grand Bay, Commonwealth of Dominica. Yvonne Laurencia came to England as a teenager and attended Lister Comprehensive in East London.

She is married and is a mother of two daughters and five grandchildren.

The author is a retired primary school teacher, nurse, midwife and health visitor.

Printed in Great Britain
by Amazon